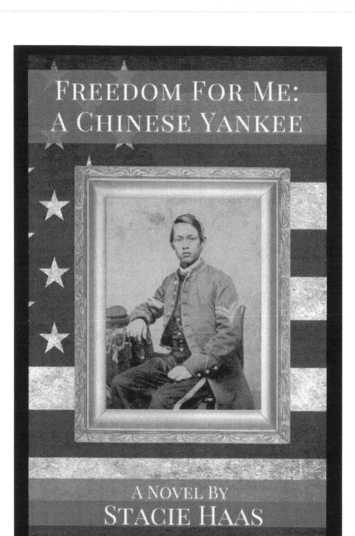

An Imprint of 50/50 Press, LLC.

Freedom For Me: A Chinese Yankee
© 2017 by Stacie Haas

For permission requests, write to the publisher, addressed "Attention: Permissions Coordinator," at the address below.

50/50 Press, LLC
PO Box 197
1590 Route 146
Rexford, NY 12148

http://www.5050press.com

ISBN-13: 978-1-947048-07-2
ISBN-10: 1-947048-07-4
Library of Congress Control Number
LCCN: 2017958950

Edited by: Stephen Hall III

This book is a work of fiction. Names, characters, places, and incidents are products of the author's imagination or are used fictitiously. The author freely discusses her inspirations for the story in the text.

For my family.

CHAPTER ONE

It was a blistering July day, the air hot and still. Seeking shade and a moment's rest under a fat, white oak tree was a Union Army private who went by the name of Thomas Beck. He was dressed in a wool frock coat, an outfit wholly unsuited for work under the blazing summer sun. But it was work he was there to do: soldier's work called *reconnaissance*, a big word for a search and find mission. It was his job to locate the Confederate troops hiding somewhere in the tired yellow wheat field.

Thomas squirmed against the thick tree trunk, trying to loosen the damp fabric from his sweaty skin. He switched the barrel of the heavy, slippery musket from one hand to another, wiping his hands on his pants leg as he went. He was distracted by that tricky maneuver when a chilling boom of cannon fire rumbled across the field.

The thundering roll echoed in his ears. Thomas instinctively grabbed hold of his queue, the long braid of twisted black hair, and ran his free hand up, down, and over. It was a move that reminded Thomas of a baby being soothed by the feel of a beloved blanket. But he didn't waste a thought being embarrassed by that. He didn't know or care which was more comforting as the battle approached: the ancient hairstyle that connected him with his ancestors, or the Sharps rifle that rested against his shoulder.

The last time Thomas had seen a queue like his own was in a different kind of field, lush and green and damp. It had belonged to the man Thomas called *Baba*, a man he'd dearly loved. *Baba's* queue had hung limp from a round bald head as men with iron hats and willow leaf swords led him away. Just a few moons old then, Thomas had hid in the slender fingers of rice paddy stalks to avoid capture.

When he took a moment to rest against the white oak, Thomas hadn't considered its value as a good hiding spot. It was certainly taller than the smooth strips of jade that swayed in the mist that day long ago, but he knew the tree was a solitary figure, a standout among vast rows of pale crops. Confederate lookouts were scanning the ground with their field glasses. They sought a flash of color, the flicker of a flag, or the fleeting wisp of smoke or powder. Infantry pickets, with their Rebel guns at arms' reach, had their ears to the ground listening for any sign of movement.

If they sensed motion by this tree, it would make an easy target for Confederate cannons.

Thomas stood ramrod straight as the cannon's rumble reached him again. Stronger this time, and louder. Thomas's heart marched a tad bit faster like the drum beats that signal battle. Maybe the old veterans had been right about him.

The old men with gray in their beards and missing teeth had shaken their heads when Thomas shot his arm into the air to volunteer for his mission like an eager student at a school house. The same men had spat and grumbled when he launched himself from the tips of his toes to get noticed by the officers.

"Hey, Tom-fool," a leathery-skinned soldier had called out. "Ya know what kind of soldier volunteers to be a skirmisher?"

"A brave and strong one?" Thomas puffed his chest.

"No," he scoffed. "A dead one."

Thomas shut his eyes against the memory. Maybe he had been a "yay-hoo" as the veteran soldiers claimed. But in his mind's eye, Thomas had seen the big, bold headline in the *Hartford Courant* re-telling his glorious role in bringing about the Civil War's final battle. Thomas fully expected to return home the pride of his Connecticut town with a lovely young lady on his arm. After all, who wouldn't want to court a war hero?

Thomas wiped sweat from his forehead, making his black hair stick to him like jam to a slice of bread. He carefully reached behind his head to push his queue into his uniform coat and peeked around the tree.

Where are you graybacks?

Beyond the crop was a large white house on a hill, overlooking a parched meadow of grasses and faded gold and brown wildflowers. A weathered barn sat east of the house, but no livestock grazed today. There was no sign of the Rebs either. No markers of their cross-hatched flag, no tall officers' hats, no clink and clunk of tin cups and metal munitions could be heard from his position.

Thomas slid down the trunk and turned, belly to the ground, toward the enemy. Tall, thick stalks stood in his way. Thomas swatted itchy weeds out of his face as he inched through the field, stirring up dust that made his dark eyes water. As he pushed through, he heard voices inside his head: his big brother ribbing him for giving battle like some lazy caterpillar; his pa's gentle but matter-of-fact way of saying you can't lead without standing up.

Thomas picked up his pace, but he doubted a fast crawl was any better than a slow one. He was getting nowhere fast. He needed to be up on his feet, at the double quick. He pictured his lieutenant back in the blue lines, tapping his foot while looking through field glasses, anxiously awaiting Thomas's report. The

Union Army of the Potomac would move on his word.

He rose to one knee. The wheat stalks were about three feet high. The men always harassed Thomas about being small, but here it could help him. At his height, Thomas could nearly stand without being seen if he bent over just a bit. Surely he could do that. He glanced at his jacket. The Southern Rebels were lucky—gray uniforms blended in better than blue.

Shrugging, Thomas found his feet and zig-zagged through the crop maze. After a spell, Thomas spread the wheat like his mama opened their parlor curtains, two sides from the middle. The house came into better view. He couldn't see past it; the landscape disappeared into a valley.

That's it—that's where the Rebs must be hiding. Thomas figured a whole company of Confederate troops was crouched at the base of the hill, just waiting for some glimpse of the enemy—of him—before bugles blared and the gray infantry marched.

Time was short. Thomas needed to confirm his suspicions and report back to his command. But first he had to make it to the house for a better look. Thomas set off with cautious steps, boxing out the nervous pops in his chest. He was close, very close to fulfilling his mission.

A violent scream penetrated Thomas's ears; the horrible, shrieking Rebel yell. Thomas dropped to his belly again, his face in the dirt.

Where are they?

He clambered fast, like a scampering mouse, as more thunder boomed across the countryside. He was in trouble now. His comrades were miles behind him and with no way to know where he was. His only way was forward. He wouldn't retreat, not now. His chest pounded.

"Surrender, soldier!"

Thomas's muscles tightened, panic shooting through him. He felt the barrel of a musket pressed into his back.

"Ah, shoot."

Thomas grunted and rolled over. He squinted into the blinding light overhead. A hearty soldier stood over him, leering.

"Darn it, Robert. How'd you find me?"

"Your braid, Tom. It's so dark. It's like a long black snake slithering in this field."

Thomas reached behind his back to find that his queue had come loose from his jacket.

"That's not fair." Thomas chucked his musket.

"Then ya shoulda got rid of it. Mama's only asked a hundred

times."

"She doesn't understand and neither do you."

"I figure that's your right, Tom, but ya lost the battle because of it." Robert whistled to mark his victory. "I can't wait to sign up tomorrow. We're gonna defeat them Rebs and save the Union."

"Mama won't let you fight."

"I'm eighteen now, remember?" Robert offered his little brother a hand.

"Then if you're going, I'm going with you—two brothers side by side." Thomas brushed the dirt and grass from his clothes.

"You're too young, and besides, there ain't no such thing as a Chinese Yankee."

"Looks like another summer heat storm is kicking up." Robert stuck a piece of wheat into his mouth as Thomas pulled on his damp shirt to let some air in. "These storms are the darnedest things, over and gone almost before they start, and violent, too. Well, at least no rain yet."

Thomas nodded, but he wasn't really listening. As the brothers ambled to their house, Thomas craned to see his six-foot-two-inch brother, bouncy blond curls stopping just shy of his big, broad shoulders.

Reaching barely beyond five feet, Thomas looked different. He had pin-straight ebony hair pulled back into a braided pigtail called a queue. The pallor of his skin looked sickly compared to his brother's summer bronzing, which somehow made Robert look even stronger and healthier than normal. And whereas his brother's eyes always twinkled blue, Thomas's pupils merged into a sea of murky brown. Robert had always jokingly admonished Thomas to stop squinting, especially when there was no sunlight to shield.

"You really think I can't fight for Connecticut, Robert?" The pair climbed a slight rise, dry wheat crunching under their feet.

"You're just a kid."

"But if I wasn't?"

"Ah, Tom. Ya know the looks ya get in town. Folks don't know what to make of ya. You're not white like us, not black, not an Indian…. Folks don't know what being Chinese means."

Neither do I, Thomas thought.

"There you boys are." A slender woman whose blond hair had

just begun to gray stood on the porch of their family home. "Who won the battle this time?"

"Robert cheated, Mama. He used my queue against me."

"I figure the enemy will use any and all means to win the war." His mama wiped two floury hands on her apron. "Come in and get washed up for supper."

After using the pump to draw water from the underground well, the boys made their way to the back of the house where they joined their mama at the square oak table. The brothers bowed their heads in prayer before attacking their mama's stew, sliding her delicious butter biscuits around the simple plate to sop up the gravy.

"I heard the army's in Hartford," Robert said between bites. "I'm gonna head on over tomorrow and sign up."

"You'll do no such thing." A pained expression spread across their mother's face. Thomas braced for a heated conversation— it's what always happened when Robert brought up the army.

"Mama, wouldn't ya have me do my duty?" Robert's voice was soft and his face was calm. Thomas's eyes opened wide in surprise.

"Your duty is here at the farm while your pa's away."

"Boys all across the North are signing up. The war's been on for a year now and they need every man." Robert breathed deep. "Mama, why read us the Scriptures or Ms. Stowe's *Uncle Tom's Cabin* book if ya didn't want me to help free the slaves?"

Thomas couldn't believe his brother's words. Robert was trying a different argument this time.

If it works, Thomas wondered, *what will happen to me?*

"President Lincoln says we're fighting to save the Union, not end slavery."

"Oh, Mama," Robert groaned. "Everyone knows what this war is really about. The South wants more slavery in America. We want less…. We want it gone. It all comes down to this."

"I won't argue with you, son. You have come of age and it's clear your mind is made up. We'll discuss it with your father when he returns from sea. Is that agreeable to you?"

"Yes, ma'am." Robert turned his head down, his voice low and burdened by disappointment. Their mama stood and cleared dishes from the table, her way of declaring the matter settled.

"What about me, Mama?" Thomas couldn't hold back. "Robert said there aren't any Chinese Yankees. Is that true?"

Mama fixed her eyes on Robert, her normally sweet expression fading as she pointed at her eldest son.

"Well, mister do-my-duty, I'll have you keep your opinion to yourself on that." She turned to Thomas. "Chinese or not, you'd make a fine Yankee soldier, if that's what you were meant to be."

"It is, ma'am. I know it is."

"You know nothing of the sort. War's no place for a boy. Your place is home."

Thomas knew not to push further. He helped dry the dishes and excused himself to finish up the day's chores. Thomas tended to the animals, milking their one cow to the rhythm of Robert chopping wood just outside the barn door. The sun had begun to set as Thomas finished clearing out the stall of their horse, Barney.

Robert hauled a pitcher full of water up to the room they shared. Thomas followed close behind carrying the fresh towels he had retrieved from the line behind the house. They took turns washing up in the basin, falling into their single bunks set across from each other. Robert punched his pillow, sending feather dust into the air.

"I'm gonna enlist tomorrow, Tom. Gonna get me some Rebs."

"You just told Mama you wouldn't do it. Not yet, anyway."

"Pa could be away for months still. Ya never know how long his water crossings will take. I'm not waiting. This is the greatest adventure that's ever gonna happen to us. Just like Great Grand Pap fought the Brits in the Revolution—now it's my turn to fight."

"Not without me." Fear coursed through Thomas like a flood, but he pushed the feeling away. "I'm going with you."

"They ain't gonna let ya join." Robert bounced out of bed, his feet landing with a heavy thump. "Even if ya were old enough, you're not a real citizen."

"Oh, yes I am, Robert." Thomas discarded his blanket and confronted his brother. "I'm just as much a citizen as you."

Thomas lay awake as his brother's snores filled the room. Even without his saying so, Thomas knew Robert planned to depart for Hartford in the middle of the night. He had just a few hours left to figure out what to do.

The floorboards felt cool on his bare feet. Desperate not to wake his mama sleeping just down the hall, Thomas shifted his weight to keep the boards from creaking. He gingerly stepped his way through the dark hall and down the stairs to the front door. He cringed at the croak that escaped when he turned the knob, but opened and closed it gently before stepping out into the dark night.

The harsh heat had disappeared with the sun, and the air was filled with a cool, gentle breeze. By instinct, Thomas knew his path, even though he couldn't see.

"Hello there, Barney." Thomas was greeted by a soft whinny as he entered the barn. "How are you, old pal? What do your horse senses tell you? Is there a war afoot?" Thomas reached out to smooth the horse's soft nose.

"I'm sure you know, don't you, old boy?" The horse blew hot breath through his nostrils. "Mama says my place is at home, but I want to do my part, too."

The horse nuzzled closer, and Thomas leaned in. He felt his way through the tack, and locating Barney's brush, groomed him with long strokes.

"Robert says the school house benches are bare," Thomas told the horse. "All the boys have joined the fight with their fathers—or they are busy making plans for when they come of age. There isn't even a question in Robert's mind about enlisting—why should there be one in mine?"

Thomas didn't want to admit that he already knew why. If he said it aloud, he would have to reckon with the sinking feeling in his chest. He rarely thought about how he was different. It was an easy thing to forget on the homestead with his pa, mama, and brother. To Thomas's mind, they were a family like any other.

His father, Joseph, was a sailor who was gone for long stretches of time so Thomas worked alongside his mama to manage their homestead while he was away. Thomas seeded and weeded their garden, worked the plow, and helped her by chopping vegetables and scrubbing clothes. When Thomas wasn't tending to their homestead, his mama read the Bible with him and taught him to read, write, and cipher.

As the older brother, Robert took care of the family's shopping, post, and other business in town after he finished his morning chores on the farm. And when Joseph was in port, Robert served as an aide to his father, the captain, when it came time to offload goods from his ship and proffer them to local merchants.

The war had changed things, even the air it seemed, on their Connecticut farm. Every day Robert returned from town with more news from Washington City and reports of the Union and Confederate armies clashing in far off places like Virginia—battles that the boys liked to recreate in their fields.

Robert brought home all manner of pamphlets, too, encouraging all men and boys of age to fight to preserve the Union; all women and girls to put their threads, needles, and prayers to work for the cause. Everyone but Thomas seemed to have a role. As Robert waited patiently to turn 18 and become a soldier, Thomas was...doing laundry.

It wasn't fair. The South had broken the country he loved into two parts and all to protect their precious slavery. He wanted to help put America back together again, and even better than before, where all men really were created equal. The Declaration of Independence's famous words should mean what they say: *all* men.

"I've got it good here, Barney." Thomas ran his fingers through the horse's mane. "I have a good family and good home and the slaves deserve that, too. That's why I should serve my country, even if I'm not a citizen in the normal way."

Thomas ran the brush down the horse hair and detangled a stubborn snag. "Looks like I'm not going to get my chance—for that or anything else. You think there's more out there than farming, pal? I'd like to join Pa's crew and sail the high seas someday. We could trade goods in China and I could see where I came from."

"I won't have any kind of life here if I can't ever leave the homestead." Thomas rested his head on the horse's flank. "I won't even hear about the happenings in town with Robert gone. There's got to be some way, somehow, to make the army accept a Chinese Yankee."

"There ain't no way." Startled, Thomas turned as Robert approached. "They ain't gonna let ya, Tom. I can just feel it."

"You leaving now?"

"Yep. Help me get Barney saddled up, will ya?"

"I don't know why I should. Why can't I come, Robert? I could at least try to convince the army that I'm a patriot who wants to help them win the war."

"It's not going to work, Tom." Robert pushed around Thomas to get Barney's blanket and saddle. "They are gonna take one look at ya and forbid it. Ya don't have to go through that."

"I say that's my choice to make."

"Tom, I'm not taking ya with me. And since I'm not, how do ya think you're gonna get to town? Ya ever walked all that way by yourself?"

Thomas felt panic rising, his chance slipping away. Barney shuffled his legs and bobbed his head, his way of protesting the bit being inserted into his mouth. The horse gave Thomas an idea.

"How about you let me ride along with you into town? You'll go on to enlist and I'll return home with Barney. Then I can try to smooth things over with Mama for you."

"Tom..."

"It's going to be hard enough on Mama to hear about you enlisting. Do you want her to try to make do without a horse, too?"

"Alright, brother," Robert relented with a shrug. "Let's get going."

CHAPTER TWO

Long before sunrise, the Beck boys mounted the old chestnut and started for Hartford. Thomas settled in behind Robert, a master horseman who knew the way to town even in the dark.

Barney picked up speed as they descended a steep hill and Thomas stiffened, forcing a chuckle from Robert. Thomas enjoyed riding, but the blackness of the night bothered him, not being able to see what was ahead.

"Give me some room, Tom, won't ya? Geez, you're gonna pull me off."

Thomas released his grip on Robert's shirttails a bit. His hold guarded against more than the bumpy, dark path. Thomas was trying to steady himself—his stomach was churning like butter.

The closer they got to town, the worse it got.

"The townspeople don't treat you any better than black folk," his mama had said once. "It's better that you stay home and focus on learning. Someday you'll be able to prove yourself as smart as them."

I don't care to be smarter, Thomas had thought. *I want to be like them, laugh at their jokes, and court a girl.*

Robert clicked his tongue against the roof of his mouth to move Barney into a faster trot. Thomas forced himself to release Robert all together and braced instead on the saddle seat. He was being a fool. He'd always been safe with his brother, and if push ever came to shove, Robert would stand up for him like no one else— except maybe their father.

The boys came to a crossroads and Thomas leaned as Robert directed the horse's reins to the left. *When Robert goes off to war,* Thomas reflected, *I will be left alone on the homestead with no hope of ever finding my own way.*

A tangerine glow filled the sky as morning dawned. The high-pitched screech of a red-tailed hawk drew Thomas's eyes up. Thomas felt a pang of jealousy over its freedom. The hawk wasn't shackled by his age, or his Chinese features, or his mama's fears. He flew above it all.

The dirt paths turned into cobblestones. Streets awoke and

store fronts opened. Thomas's heart quickened as cheerful music reached his ears. The town's energy reminded him of the jovial brass band whose bugles, fifes, and drums whistled pride-stirring American hymns as it passed by their homestead on the last Fourth of July.

In the middle of town, Center Church was adorned in red, white, and blue. American flags flanked each side of the square building; festive bunting wrapped its roof ledge. Its tall, white steeple reached to the heavens beckoning Connecticut's young men to enlist in the cause. In the town green, a rotund man in a tailored suit and tall hat readied to make a speech.

Robert cantered to the post office. He vaulted off and tied the horse's reins while Thomas dismounted. The boys started toward the gathering crowd.

"This has got to be the place." Robert clapped his hands and smacked his lips. He sprinted to the church. Thomas scurried to keep up.

"Hey there, Fred," Robert shouted. "William, fancy meeting you here."

Thomas nudged his brother, eager to meet the two boys featured in Robert's frequent town adventure stories.

"Oh, Fred and William, this is Thomas, my—" Thomas's smile diminished as Robert went on, "—he lives with us." An invisible force slapped Thomas on the face.

"Um, yes," Thomas managed, rubbing his cheek against the cotton on his shoulder to soften the blow. "It's an honor to make your acquaintance."

Thomas extended his hand, saw looks of surprise and disgust, and withdrew. He smoothed the other cheek.

"President Abraham Lincoln," the fat man in the suit began, "having ordered an additional 300,000 troops hereby calls on you to defend Connecticut and the Constitution of the United States against the Southern Rebels actively engaged in acts of insurrection—"

"They're signing people up." Robert pointed. "Let's go." His friends started off, but before he left, Robert turned.

"Tom, ya go on home to Mama now. The horse knows the way. Ya tell her I'm sorry and that I'll make her proud."

"Robert, I want to come, too." Thomas swallowed the hurt.

"Ya can't. Look, I'm sorry, but those boys are fools and they won't understand me having a Chinese brother. The army is gonna be the same way and won't let ya fight. It ain't right, but that's how it is. Please go home. I'll be there before ya know it— just after we lick them Rebs."

Thomas and Robert shook hands and they stayed linked for a

long moment to mark their farewell. Robert nodded to his brother and Thomas's eyes followed him as he took his place in the line.

Thomas stood motionless in the street. He ignored the angry yells of people steering their horses and wagons around him. He could do nothing but stare at the recruiting station, watching as waves of men and boys went in and came out, one after another, doing what he longed to do: volunteer to serve his country.

Robert emerged from the recruitment building some time later with a broad smile and enlistment papers in hand. He played soldier with his friends, modeled guns with his fingers, and pretended to fall when hit by imaginary bullets.

With his path set, Robert disappeared from Thomas's sight, headed off to fight for a country that apparently didn't want Thomas's services. Despair clung to Thomas like a wet blanket. The Beck family war games would soon be real for Robert, while Thomas stayed behind. He felt like the war had already been lost.

The fat man spoke under an open rotunda on the green, his talk returning to the events that led to the Great War between the States.

"Slavery wrought this war," Thomas's mother had said, clutching her Bible, just after the fighting started. "Nothing good could ever come from one people enslaving another. It's a shameful disgrace in a country founded on freedom."

Thomas had nodded his agreement. He didn't know any slaves, but like many other Northerners, he had read Harriet Beecher Stowe's book about life under slavery. Instead of Robert's *McGuffey Reader* from school, Thomas's mama had used *Uncle Tom's Cabin* for his lessons. When Thomas had an occasion to consider slavery, he thought of Uncle Tom and his brutal master, Simon Legree.

"It ain't about slavery, boys," his father had chimed in. "It's about whether the South can leave the Union when they ain't happy. They got upset about Abe Lincoln's election—a fair and square democratic election—so they up and quit. It's a crying shame. We'll fight to preserve America as one country."

"Darn straight, Pa." Robert had slapped his knee. "What do ya think, Tom?"

Thomas had shrugged. Slavery was hard to reckon, but the idea of an entire country out there befuddled him. Thomas's allegiance would always be with his home, and his was in the North, in the United—not the so-called Confederate—States of America.

"I don't think the South can fire their guns on a US fort and not expect us to fight back," Thomas had reasoned.

"Aye, Thomas." His father had risen from his rocking chair to stoke the fire. "We're not going to stand pat."

That's what I'm doing now, Thomas thought, *standing pat*. He turned at the sound of a woman crying behind him. A mother held her son in her arms, wishing him a safe return. Thomas thought of his own mother, Madeline, who desperately wanted to shelter her sons from life beyond their homestead—one from the big war and the other from the war she knew would meet Thomas wherever he went.

"Oh, Mama," Thomas murmured. "I ought to come home and help you while Robert and Pa are away. I'll be fine, right?" he asked her, as if she could hear him. Thomas let the decision settle in his heart for a moment. Soon it formed a lump in his throat.

"Yes, mighty fine," he said aloud, not caring who heard him. "Fine like a caged animal is fine until he realizes there's life beyond the cage he can't reach."

Thomas closed his eyes and breathed deep. *Just get on the horse and go home,* Thomas ordered himself. Simple as that. It's what everyone expected. He'd do right by his mama, be obedient to his pa, and submit to Robert. But then what?

Thomas opened his eyes and let his breath go. He found Robert engaged in conversation with a group of boys. Careful not to be seen, Thomas approached.

"So that boy with you," a burly, barrel-chested redhead said, "what was he, a slave your father brought home from sea?"

Shock rooted Thomas in his place.

"He's a good boy, Henry." Robert fidgeted with his hands.

"I'll bet he is." Henry's face lit up. "I gotta hand it to your pa. He's mighty smart—genius really."

"What nonsense are ya speaking, Henry?"

"Why, your secret slave. No slavery allowed anywhere's here in the North, so your pa sails over to another country—what did ya call it? China?—to get ya'll one. I ain't never heard tell about him and wouldn't nobody ever find out on your homestead. How does he do?"

"Beg your pardon?" Robert's head snapped up.

"He don't look as strong as them other slaves—kinda puny—but I bet he does alright for your mama. You wanna barter for him? Maybe he could come along to the war, carry my knapsack, and cook my grub." Henry winked. "I'd probably make him cut that long braid, though. Seems like it'd get in the way. Anyways, I'd treat him real nice."

"If ya take him along," Robert reasoned, "he wouldn't be so

secret anymore, now would he?"

A scorching heat rose in Thomas's face and spread throughout his frame. He clenched his fists as he tore away from the group.

Slave!

These boys think I'm a Beck family slave. And Robert—who is he, the son of my master? He's certainly not my brother. My brother would have said something—anything—to correct Henry.

Thomas strode back and forth, rage filling him. He darted into an alley between the mercantile and Center Church, stomping so hard that a stray cat scrambled to get out of his way. He paced until sweat beaded and his anger tempered. His feet slowed as his anger turned into disappointment.

How can that boy look at me and assume I'm a slave? Sure, I don't resemble Robert or any of the other boys joining up. I'm not black like the slaves, either. We are in Hartford, Connecticut. We're in the North and the Union. There's no slavery here! Why, oh why, does this Henry think I'm a slave? Is it my queue? My black hair and slanted eyes? The way I talk?

Is this what it feels like to be a slave?

Thomas rubbed his face with his hands. He had only been presumed to be a slave, yet the air had been sucked out of him like he'd been punched. It was shocking and awful for him to realize that slavery being outlawed in the North didn't mean that black people were accepted, or wanted, or...equal. This was not how Thomas figured life in America was supposed to be.

All this time, Thomas presumed that his home in the North was a safe-haven, a friendly and accepting place. Maybe that was just his homestead, and his mama had been right. It was clear to Thomas now that not all Northerners felt strongly against the terrible institution. Still, it was a fact that the North was fighting to keep slavery from spreading into the western territories, while the South was fighting to expand it.

When did everything get so complicated? Thomas scratched his head. Robert was surely right that he should have never come to Hartford.

Slowly building from a simmer into a boil, Thomas's anger began to return until it flamed red hot. No—things weren't going to change by sitting around and waiting for it. Thomas wasn't a slave, but for the first time, he got a tiny inkling about how they felt and it was worse than he ever imagined.

Thomas suddenly had trouble remembering the comfortable life he'd had with the Becks. With that one word—slave—Thomas started questioning everything he knew: how he'd been brought to America, his mama's rules, and even his chores and how they differed from Robert's. Questions clouded his head. Answers were slow to come, but Thomas knew one thing.

"If I'm a soldier then I can't be a slave," Thomas muttered aloud, pacing again in the street. "I have to find a way to fight."

Because a fight sounded good just then—with anyone who cared to pick one.

Thomas darted to the line forming at the door. Boys ahead of him giggled and laughed, obviously up to something. A boy who looked much younger than him scribbled "18" on a piece of paper and placed it in the bottom of his shoe so the number would be under his foot.

Thomas's head jerked up with understanding. He tore a piece of cloth from his haversack and asked to borrow their pencil. They shot him a strange look but handed it over.

"One problem down," Thomas muttered under his breath. Knots bunched in his belly while he waited. This had to work. Finally, he found himself standing in front of an officer.

"Name?" the officer asked, not looking up.

"Thomas Beck, sir."

"Age?"

"I am *over* eighteen, sir," Thomas declared.

"Sure you are." The officer beheld Thomas, and his smile faded. "What are you doing here, boy?" The officer slammed his fist on the table.

"Sir." Thomas gulped, willing his voice to speak. "I am a resident of Connecticut, son of Joseph and Madeline Beck. I am here to enlist in the Union Army and crush the Southern rebellion."

Laughter erupted behind the table where three officers sat. Thomas stood firm and pretended not to hear, hoping the table hid the quake in his legs. When the noise died down, Thomas heard one officer whisper to another.

"I suppose he can stop a bullet as good as a white man," the officer said, his lips forming into a sly smile.

"Can't argue that," the other officer agreed.

"Congratulations, boy." The first officer handed Thomas the papers. "You are a private in the Fourteenth Regiment Connecticut Volunteer Infantry."

Thomas tried not to let loose the big grin that threatened to escape. He was a soldier, a Yankee, ready to fight for the North. He rushed out the door.

Merry boys jammed the street, celebrating in concert with the band's trumpet blasts and drum beats. Thomas turned all the way around, searching, scanning for Robert.

His brother stood just off to his right, behind the town livery, with the same boys as before—his friends, Fred and William, and Henry, the redhead who thought Thomas was a slave. Thomas stood tall and bounced on his tiptoes toward them.

His brother's back was to him. Thomas tapped him on the shoulder, and Robert swung around.

"Tom, what in creation ya still doing here?"

"I'm going with you, brother."

"Are my ears making fits, or did he say he was your brother?" Henry chortled, bending over and slapping his thigh. Howls of laughter filled the space.

"You, Henry, go on and hush. Get out of here." Robert's face turned red, the way it always did when he got his dander up.

Henry moved backwards, still caught up in the hee-haw of his laughter, pulling Fred and William off with him.

"What are ya talking about, Tom?" Robert shouted, a spray of spit landing on Thomas's cheek.

"I enlisted, brother." Thomas wiped the spit with the back of his hand. "We're going off to war together. Like I told you, I'm a citizen too."

Robert became a statue, silent and unmoving. Thomas could see he was fuming and readied himself for a storm of angry words. His brother's temper was legendary.

"What's gonna happen now, Tom?" Robert's voice fell to a whisper as he bent over and leaned in close. "You think these boys are gonna be happy to see ya join up? How am I gonna fight if I'm always watching over your hide?"

"I don't need you to take care of me, brother." Thomas's words were shaky. He'd never figured on a whisper having more power than a shout. He cleared his throat. "I'm a soldier now too."

"And Mama? What about Pa? Ya think about them?"

"Did you, Robert?" Thomas countered. "You promised Mama you'd stay home until Pa returned. I told her no such thing."

"It's not gonna be easy for ya," Robert grumbled. "Or me neither." His brother's face resumed its angry red, and his voice pitched higher. "Did ya think of me when ya decided to become a soldier?" He pointed to Fred, William, and Henry. "What are they going to think?"

"I'm more interested in what you think, Robert. Are we brothers or not?"

"What are ya talking about, Tom?"

"I'd think my brother would be happy for me—for us. We get to share the adventure now—not on the farm, but for real. Or do you think Henry's right and Pa only meant for me to be your secret slave?"

Robert grimaced. He kicked the ground with the toe of his boot and shook his head.

"Just gimme time, Tom."

"But Robert—"

"A little time alone, Tom. Will ya do that for me?"

When his brother marched away, Thomas had no choice but to turn in the opposite direction. He faced a rowdy crowd of fresh-faced soldiers reveling in the green. Long lines of men and boys spilled over from Center Church where enlistments were continuing.

"Darn army must be desperate hiring Indians for this fight—look at that long black hair—might as well be an Indian." Thomas heard as he passed by Henry, Fred, and William who were gathered with their heads together.

"Nah, he's no Indian," Henry joined. "His pigtail's braided all fancy-like. He's some kind of fancy Chinese slave."

Thomas hastened his steps and wriggled through the horde, praying that the group wouldn't follow. He could hear their snickers and whispers. When at last he found some open space in the street, he stole a careful look behind him and saw no sign of them. He took a deep calming breath and glanced up to see the shingle of a barber shop.

Thomas touched the tight twists of his queue as he stepped up a stair plank. At just six years old, Thomas's braid had been only a few inches long when he came to America. Joseph, his new American pa, had told him that all Chinese men and boys wore their hair in a queue because of the emperor's rules. Thomas had decided then to let his queue grow like the one his baba wore. In his heart, Thomas had become an American the moment he'd stepped from Joseph's great ship, but he didn't want to forget where he'd come from.

But if I don't have it anymore, maybe then..., Thomas shook off the thought. His hair wasn't the true cause of his trouble.

Thomas made his way to the wood-planked exterior wall of the barber shop, just outside of the crowd. The scent of fried chicken and potatoes, sweet fruit pies, and warm bread wafted across his nose. Thomas imagined spreading fresh butter across a piece of that bread. He could almost hear the scrape of its hearty crust and feel its velvety-soft inside.

The whole town was a picnic. Thomas could hear the cheery bands, smell the baked treats, and observe the hearty handshakes, but he stood a step apart like an uninvited party guest.

CHAPTER THREE

Thomas passed his first night as a Union soldier sleeping under the stars. There were no tents, no uniforms, and no organized marches. The only order was to stay in town during the day and wait for a steamer ship that would take them to the war.

The infantry was a strange mix of salty sailors, homesteaders, farmers, and merchants who pranced around in buttoned suits with dangling pocket watch chains. There were old men and young men, and to Thomas's surprise, many who looked even younger than he. Thomas was several years shy of enlistment age, but the boys who tapped the drums in the infantry band looked too young to mount a horse.

Thomas longed for company. Many of the fresh enlistments were surrounded by all manner of kin—fathers, mothers, sisters, and brothers—even the family mutt trailed some of the newly-minted Union soldiers. He searched for Robert, but it was clear his brother was avoiding him. Thomas watched as a silver-haired father with a hitch in his step guided his son around town, his arm draped affectionately across his boy's shoulders, speaking into his ear.

Thomas cringed. He could use a huge heap of his father's wisdom right about now. Joseph could always steer Thomas in the right direction when he lost his way. If he were here, Joseph would remind Thomas that he chose this path and it was up to him to set about doing something good with it, no matter how hard it was.

"I reckon you made your bed, my boy. Now, you'll be lying in it."

Thomas could hear his father's words clearly in his head. Joseph would be cheerful, but serious and true all the same. He'd offer Thomas a firm pat on the back with a knowing smile on his lips.

Thomas's heart felt heavy as he watched a mother fret over her son's shirt, her small hands smoothing its wrinkles. Thomas ached as he thought of his mama. By now she'd know her sons had enlisted against her wishes. He and Robert hadn't even said goodbye. Thomas felt a deep pang of regret. He had told Robert that he'd return home to her to explain his brother's actions.

Thomas had enlisted against his word. He'd been moved to fight injustice and instead, had done an injustice against his own mother.

Thomas needed to find Robert. He searched for him on Main Street and considered how different horse hooves sounded on cobblestones than on the farm—that, and how much harder to avoid their odorous droppings. Thomas took a deep breath, inhaled past the manure to discern the delicious scents of virgin's bower, trillium, and merry bell flowers growing along the street. That was better. Now where was his brother?

Thomas wandered under store-front awnings, peered through their windows, hoping to find Robert shopping. He paused in front of the magnificent state house with its elegant white columns and ornate clock tower. When he looked away, Thomas spotted Robert jawing with a group of boys. He caught his brother's eye, but Robert pretended not to see him, looking past him.

When other boys stared or called out their insults, Thomas gritted his teeth. But he struggled to hide his hurt when Robert rebuffed him. It was like being turned through a grist mill. Thomas wished for an opportunity to apologize for breaking his word, and he wanted Robert to reassure him of their kinship. But, although they were constantly near each other, Robert chose not to acknowledge Thomas's presence.

Thomas turned right on State Street, the water beckoning him. He sat on the bank near the massive ships, their tall masts reaching skyward, their white sails like oversized sheets flapping in the breeze.

Joseph was out there somewhere, beyond the calm waters, in the deep, blue ocean. He'd be at the helm, navigating the waves. Once his crew had docked in a faraway land, he'd trade with the native peoples.

Robert had dripped with excitement after his first voyage with their father and regaled his brother with colorful stories of peoples, sights, and smells. Thomas could only dream of it. He'd only asked to accompany his father once. The 'no' he'd gotten was flat and piercing, a sharp contrast to the usual brimming of Joseph's lavish affection. His mama had said it was for his protection, but Thomas didn't understand why.

It was a fact that Thomas didn't understand much of anything at the moment. He had left his mother alone on the farm. His brother didn't want to speak with or even acknowledge him in front of the other soldiers. Thomas only knew he hated the idea of slavery—and anything close to it—and that he wanted to help his country live up to its potential. He wanted to find some way to live up to his, too.

Thomas peered out into the distance, ripples moving in little waves. His thoughts drifted back to the last time he looked out upon the water. It had been ten years since Thomas arrived in America.

Thomas was born in a different water town, a deep sea port on the Zhu Jiang delta called Kuangchou in southern China. One day after the Chinese New Year, young Thomas sat atop his uncle's shoulders on a bank overlooking the South China Sea. He'd been instructed to search for red- and blue-striped flags on the sterns of ships at the water's edge. With his tiny hand perched above his brow, Thomas's eyes squinted to see, the rising sun shrouding the flags in a dense fog.

"Where are we going, *Shushu*?" Thomas asked in his native Chinese that morning, rubbing the sleep from his eyes.

"You are embarking on a long journey." His uncle hastily placed a cap on Thomas's head. "Come, come."

They had a good vantage point for witnessing great numbers of workers below. Big men with flaxen and auburn hair, scraggly beards, and husky chests unloaded goods from massive vessels, bellowing words Thomas didn't recognize to workers on land. Other men traded for goods and exchanged monies.

Thomas watched a group of Chinese men and boys, their heads down, board a ship single-file. That ship had a flag with one white stripe flanked by two red ones, which his American father would later teach him was the flag of Peru.

"There." Thomas pointed to two ships, one flying the British Union Jack, the other featuring the stars and stripes of America.

Shushu's hands clasped around Thomas's tiny waist, pulled him down, and grabbed his hand with a force Thomas didn't expect. They sprinted through a maze of men. Dark shapes whizzed across Thomas's eyes, the smell of sweat mixed with salty sea air rushing by his nose. Breathlessly, uncle and nephew reached one of the red- and blue-flagged ships. His uncle ran to a stack of wooden crates similarly decorated, ready to be capped and loaded. Before hoisting Thomas into one, his uncle turned to him.

"Be silent, child, until you get onboard."

"*Shushu,* I'm not going in there—"

His uncle stomped his foot and his queue flapped hard against his silk coat. Fire flickered in his black eyes stemming young Thomas's protest.

"You must go." *Shushu* patted the top of his head. "It's for your safety. I made a promise to your *baba* before he was taken from the fields. Your father implored me to protect you and I will honor his request. Go."

Thomas shuddered at the memory of the wooden crate, how he'd wedged himself into a corner to brace himself as it was suspended in mid-air, then landed with a muted thud on the ship deck. The crate's dark interior was illuminated with tiny beams of light glowing through small cracks. At regular intervals, the box darkened for a moment, deck hands passing by. Thomas kicked the boards to alert them to his presence, yelled as loud as his lungs could muster, his fear of the crate overriding his fear of discovery.

The boy's clothes, soaked in sweat and wet with tears, clung to him and made him shiver. His voice abandoned him as time wore on, but his foot continued to thrust. The repeated thwack on the boarded wall brought the boy a small measure of relief, something he could control. The rhythm was somewhat soothing.

The boy's head lifted when sunshine poured through the crate, its cover removed. Thomas heard a deep and friendly voice.

"Well, what have we got here?"

Thomas wore a sheepish look when he glanced up and beheld Joseph Beck's face. Warm, twinkling eyes smiled down on him and he couldn't help but smile back. Joseph lunged at Thomas with his big, strong arms and held the wet lad in his arms. Two months later, they arrived in these waters of the Connecticut

Sound.

The memories of his father and the cool water breezes calmed Thomas as he rested his eyes. He wished for nightfall. Last night, as he slept, Thomas dreamt that his brother was with him. He even thought he felt his head being lifted but knew it could not be since Robert was avoiding him.

But sure enough, when he awoke in the morning, he found his brother's haversack was under his head and there were more coins in his trouser pocket. Robert was taking care of him when no one could see, even Thomas himself.

When the distant drums of the infantry sprang to life, calling him back into the present day and time, Thomas was keenly aware that it was daylight.

"Men," a mustached soldier on horseback shouted, a bugle blaring. "I am Lieutenant George Pierce. We are moving out."

Blue-clad officers hollered orders as sergeants used their arms like horse pens to corral the men into columns of four. Bubbles of nervousness burst in Thomas's chest. A fervent need to get close to Robert compelled him through the crowd. If only the sergeant would form them into a column together. Vomit rose in Thomas's throat when a big arm restrained him, bumping him into slave-minded Henry.

"Darn China boy," Henry grumbled.

Turning his back, Henry shook hands with a bearded man with bad teeth who said his name was James. The sergeant rustled another boy to them. He looked young like Thomas, tall and thin with a soft, clear face, straw-colored hair falling into his eyes. Thomas sensed a friendly soul but couldn't muster the courage to offer him a greeting.

They were lined up so close that their shoulders were touching. Or they should have been. James had to be six foot, the others shorter. But all towered above Thomas. His head bumped into Henry's bulky arms and the lanky ones of the skinny kid, whose name was Elias.

Another bugle blared: orders to move out. An awkward march, in groups of four, commenced. Thomas tried to match the strides of the bigger soldiers, but he felt slight, like a toddler in a parade of men. And men who looked nothing like him.

For a brief moment, Thomas wished he could look more like his family. Oh, how great it would be to have five more inches, fair hair, and a pointed nose. If only he'd inherited his family through the bloodline like Robert. He could look like Pa, strong and brave, and then maybe they'd notice him.

Or better yet, Thomas recalled their taunts in Hartford, *maybe they'll just let me be.*

CHAPTER FOUR

Thomas held a tin cup, steam rising from a dark, murky liquid inside. He breathed in the aroma, like burnt biscuits, not sure about taking a sip. All the soldiers drank coffee, so Thomas studied the men, imitated them.

He had grabbed a handful of smooth brown beans from a barrel in front of the mess tent and dropped them in a tin can with a clink. He crushed the beans with a skinny rock until a gritty powder formed and then added some water from a nearby running stream. Using a long stick, Thomas suspended the boiler from its wire bail and held it above the campfire. When the water bubbled and blackened and steamed, it was finished.

His first cup burned down his throat and tasted like bark. He missed his mama's sweet apple cider but said "ah" and "that hits the spot" like the other men.

Thomas was considering a second cup when a bugle sounded. Ever since they arrived at Camp Foote, two miles outside of Hartford, rumors about uniforms had dashed through camp. Thomas hoped this was the moment. He sprinted to grab a place in line, jumped forward when an officer shouted, "Beck, Thomas."

Thomas beamed when an aide handed him a bundle. First the coffee, now this. Wearing a uniform would make Thomas look like everyone else, and he couldn't wait. He darted to a hearty mulberry bush and ripped through the paper. He removed blue trousers first. He discarded his pants and slid them on, hastily fastening the buttons. They were loose around his waist and Thomas held them in place with one hand while he searched for braces—suspenders—with the other.

"Yes." Thomas was delighted. He fastened the braces onto his pants and over his shoulders: still too big, but they'd stay with some finagling. Thomas was too excited to care.

He pulled on the heavy blue wool frockcoat. He felt like a tiny bug in a big blanket, but the brass buttons shined in the sun. He positioned his cap on his head, and it fell down over his eyes. Pushing it up with his pointer finger, he marched in place, knees high.

The next bugle signaled the issuing of muskets, and Thomas

couldn't keep still. He felt like a soldier, and he wondered if what he felt, this joy mixed with trembling, was what it was like before a battle. He pondered if this feeling was why he decided to enlist against everyone's wishes, why it mattered more than hurting his mother and his brother. It was all to be this: a soldier serving his country.

Properly outfitted and armed, the Fourteenth Connecticut Infantry set out to learn drill and ceremony. Thomas's legs ached and his arms wearied with each day of drill. In his sleep, he heard his Irish sergeant shouting commands.

"Attention."

"Dress, right, dress."

"Front."

"Right face."

"Forward march."

"Company halt."

The troops had competently mastered marching in a column of

fours, but moving into a battle line proved harder. Thomas toed the mark, determined to be faster and better than the others. There was no way he would give the men another reason to call him out.

But they did anyway.

"Look at that slave in a fighting suit," Henry shouted, "trying to show us up in the field. C'mon China boy, slow down there. Ain't no battle up ahead."

Henry, bearded James, and skinny Elias were Thomas's tent mates. When not drilling, they were assigned fatigue duties—cooking, chopping firewood, erecting corrals for the officers' horses—and shared a big camp tent. Neither Thomas nor Henry liked the arrangement. Henry had claimed his sleeping spot near the tent opening, closest to the fire's light. In return, Thomas placed his bedroll on the far side, furthest from him. Still, Henry never passed on an opportunity to harass Thomas.

One evening after drill, Henry gathered with a group of men for a card game. Thomas passed by, hoping to make it to the tent unseen. The voices grew louder.

"Hey fellas, you ever wonder why a slave is of more use to the army than them Chinese Yankee boys?" Henry called.

The group looked over the fanned cards in their fingers, smirks crossing their faces.

"Tell us, Henry," one called out.

"At least a slave's got muscles and a strong back like an ox—not a little girl's body with a pretty little pigtail."

The boys howled, some throwing down their cards. Henry snickered and stared Thomas down. Thomas stiffened his back, pretended not to hear. He fought the urge to touch his queue.

Safely cloaked behind the tent flaps, Thomas relaxed his shoulders and let out a sigh. He thought of Joseph. He hoped, if his father were here, he would not be disappointed in the way he was handling Henry's insults.

His father always said that every man's life was beset by stormy seas at one time or another, but the wise sailor was the one who kept his eyes fixed on the horizon and navigated through the waves with a calm, clear head.

Thomas pictured a beautiful orange horizon ahead of him every time Henry spewed his hateful words. He refused to flinch when eager eyes were upon him, waiting for him to react. Although filled with a growing rage, Thomas quieted his thoughts, imagined his uniform coat was a shield that deflected their comments. Only Thomas knew that they actually penetrated his invisible defenses and caused him great distress.

Thomas wanted to be able to talk with Robert, but he hadn't seen hide nor hair from him in days. Robert could help Thomas, if only his brother would stop avoiding him and acknowledge his existence. It was painful to see Robert every day, and also to feel so distant from him. Thomas was determined to wait it out, knowing he would come around eventually. He always did.

Thomas settled in to rest. Live firing exercises commenced the next day. Thomas couldn't wait. He already knew how to fire the musket—it was like his rifle at home, the one his father had taught him how to hunt with, even if Robert got that duty more often than him. Weapons training wouldn't be like learning army maneuvers from scratch—Thomas already had a leg up and a chance to prove his mettle.

Thank goodness, Thomas grinned, for those quick-darting squirrels on the farm. They made small, fast targets—excellent teachers of marksmanship. Delicious, too. Thomas licked his lips at a warm memory.

"Aye, son, you sure peppered your Mama's old rag with holes," Pa had said on their farm, examining the cloth after Thomas had handed it to him. "But far as I can tell, it wasn't doing much moving tacked onto that fence post. Robert's in town about now, so I think it's time for you to earn your supper."

With his rifle in hand, Thomas had eagerly followed his father to the wooded area that flanked their fields. Joseph looked to the high branches in the trees and pointed out a plump squirrel. Thomas aimed and fired, but the shot only alerted the squirrel to skedaddle. So did Thomas's next five shots.

"It takes a keen eye, but you'll learn to spot them. Once you do, look ahead. Don't shoot where they are, but where you expect them to go. You keep at it. I'm working up quite a hunger."

Thomas was miffed as he watched his father walk away. He was even more so when Robert returned an hour later saying he was starving. It took the better part of the evening, but as the last remnants of the sun sank into darkness, Thomas entered their house with six skinned squirrels and dropped them into his mama's pot. His brother had clapped and hollered, but his father had said nothing. He remained in his chair, a silent smile spreading across his face.

The next morning, soldiers lined up with their muskets at shoulder arms, awaiting their sergeant's commands:

"Prepare to load."

"Load."

"Handle cartridge."

"Tear cartridge."

Thomas tore into the cartridge with his teeth, poured the powder down the barrel of the musket, and seated the Minie ball. He rammed the ball down, replaced the rammer, and cocked the weapon when the sergeant shouted, "prime." Then he returned his musket to shoulder arms to await the order to fire.

He finished his task long before the others. Robert did, too. Thomas drew satisfaction knowing that the Beck brothers—though few had made that connection—could handle their weapons.

Henry struggled. He couldn't get the cartridge opened. He drew the rammer clumsily and took altogether too long to load his musket.

"You, Private Marshall, you ever handle a rifle before, boy-o?" the sergeant barked into Henry's face. "You telling me that Private Beck here, a little Chinaman, can load a gun faster than you?"

Henry clenched his teeth and stomped his foot. He moved faster as the sergeant's commands grew louder, but he dropped the rammer, cursed, and bent over to retrieve it.

"Must the entire regiment wait for you, boy-o? I suppose we could ask old Robert E. Lee to halt his advance. Heck, let's just call off the war, huh, boy-o?"

Henry darted his head to Thomas, his hands tightening into a fist. He mumbled under his breath through clenched teeth.

"You'll pay for this, China boy!"

A ginger sunset cast a beautiful glow across the landscape. For the first time in a long while—maybe since he'd enlisted—Thomas felt exuberant and light. Firing his musket had renewed his strength, and he hadn't felt strong since he joined up.

Maybe he wasn't the typical Northern soldier, but his uniform and weapon fooled him into feeling like one. The time to prove it to everyone would soon come. He had almost felt sorry for Henry on the firing range—*almost.*

Thomas meandered around camp. His tent mates chatted and sang around the fire in the evenings, but Thomas had not been invited. And he wasn't one to invite himself. He had hoped to get to know Elias in some way, speak with him, but Henry's mean glares discouraged him from trying.

Instead, Thomas ducked inside the tent each night, reviewed the day's drill in his head and scribed notes. Then he penned a letter to his mama by candlelight. But tonight's writing could wait. With a spring in his step and a jovial smile plastered on his round face, Thomas ambled through the tents.

"Oh, Robert," Thomas hummed, his voice low enough only he could hear his words, "where are you, brother?"

Thomas felt sure Robert looked for him, too, as exciting as the firing range was. He wished to go over it with him like they used to at home. After their mock battles, the boys dissected their strategies while lying in bed. It had drawn out their fun long past sundown.

Robert's tent, the one he shared with Fred and William, was anchored just a few tents down from his own, but his brother wasn't anywhere to be seen. Thomas snapped his fingers. He was thankful the sun had set—the darkness hid him in plain sight. How nice to walk without the ribbing and insults—it was just one more thing to feel good about tonight.

Thomas took another tack, his first search yielding nothing. He dashed behind the tents, thinking Robert may have visited the latrines down the hill. A faint odor wafted by Thomas's nose. He crinkled it. The smell wasn't what he expected. It was smoky, but not like a campfire burning hickory and spruce and oak. He turned toward muffled sounds of voices and saw an orange-red ember floating in front of him.

Thomas executed a flanking movement—*hooray, the drill was taking seed*—so he could approach unheard. He gasped at the sight before him. Robert was smoking a cigar.

His brother made his lips like a fish in water, bobbing open and closed on the thick, pencil-shaped log, and coughed as smoke rose from its end. He passed the smoking cylinder to William, who shared it with Fred. Thomas shook his head. What on earth was Robert thinking? Mama would tan his hide.

"Think I'm gonna take this back to camp," William proclaimed. "Show them other Connecticut men how it's done."

"I'll wrestle you for it." Robert swore, punched William playfully in the arm.

"So this is what you'd rather do than spend time with me," Thomas said beneath his breath. He turned, deciding to leave his brother to his shenanigans. He slumped back to the tent and slipped in quietly from behind. He lit his candle, retrieved his paper, and settled down to dip his pen.

"Thomas," Henry called. "Come on out and join us."

Alarm bells erupted in Thomas's head at the sound of Henry's voice, but he sounded friendly. When he called Thomas a second time, his tone was even kinder, if a bit eager.

Has something changed? Did I impress him with my skills with the musket?

Henry called again with no trace of the meanness or ribbing of all the times before. Thomas began to hope that tonight he would feel the fire's warmth.

Thomas pushed the tent flap aside and stepped out, saw a group of men huddled together. He stepped to them but then stumbled backwards, a fist landing square on his jaw. Thomas shook the cobwebs and shock away.

What is happening here?

Pairs of hands grabbed his overcoat and pulled him back up. Another punch landed in Thomas's gut. A searing pain spread in his belly, doubling him over. He could feel nothing but the hurt, blow by painful blow. He wanted to fight back, but there was no time to recover between punches and kicks.

"Robert, help me!"

The attack continued hard and fast, Thomas shrieking from agonizing blows to his chest, stomach, and legs. He didn't know who was attacking him. The figures were lost in a blur of bashes and blood.

A lieutenant came over to break up the fight, but by then, Thomas's body lay still in anguish. His flesh was tender, wounds raw, excruciating stabs pricked his limbs. The world collapsed around Thomas, his body an apt spokesperson for his will. He'd never had the chance to fight back, and now he'd lost his strength.

The lieutenant ordered two sergeants to carry Thomas to the medical tent. His wounds were tended in silence, the surgeon shaking his head as he dabbed away the blood and dirt and placed white cloth bandages over the cuts. When he was alone on a cot, angry tears spilled out of Thomas's eyes. He wiped them away defiantly.

Henry will not defeat me! I deserve to be here as much as he does. He won't win against me any more than the South will win this dang war. Not if I have anything to say about it.

CHAPTER FIVE

Thomas winced as he stepped from the hospital tent two days later. It hurt to walk, every motion a chore, pain radiating from head to foot. Staying on sick call after his row with Henry would help him heal, but Thomas couldn't do it. He wouldn't shirk his duty like a coward. Besides, that would give Henry the satisfaction of beating him with more than his fists.

"They sent word back home weeks ago that we'd be moving out." Two soldiers passed Thomas and went on by the tent rows toward a grassy knoll.

"Think we'll head straight to battle?" one asked.

"Lousy graybacks better watch out if we do."

Thomas followed the pair with slow, deliberate steps, careful not to headline his pain. Lieutenant Pierce was speaking to a gathering of men.

"Ready yourselves, Yanks. The elephant awaits."

Thomas blew out his breath.

Are we really heading straight to our first battle? How long did I sleep?

The lieutenant ordered the regiment to prepare for a military review and formal send-off. Orders were dispensed to each private to clean his uniform and report.

Thomas's hand flew to his face to feel the effects of the beating. A disheveled man with long gray whiskers and gaunt cheeks motioned to him, handed him a piece of looking glass. Thomas nodded his thanks, convinced that the man had long stopped caring what he looked like.

Thomas turned his head down and made fast tracks to his tent. A big body stepped in his path, strong arms grabbing him.

"Tom!" Robert's face grimaced, shock and anger registering. "What happened to ya? Who did this?"

"I wouldn't want to trouble you, brother." Thomas removed himself from Robert's grasp and stepped back gingerly.

"Oh, Tom, I'm sorry. I didn't know. I wasn't—"

"There." Thomas finished his brother's sentence. "You weren't there. Not since we joined up." Thomas noticed Fred and William coming up through the grass lane between the tents.

"I'll leave you to your friends. Perhaps they have another cigar." Thomas saw Robert's bewildered look and forced himself to walk away.

Guilt engulfed Thomas as he stepped inside the empty tent. Perhaps he should have been more forgiving, but every ache in his body was a reminder that Robert had abandoned him.

Thomas noticed the glass in his hand and took an uneasy glance at his reflection. The image startled him. The flesh around his eyes had a bluish-purple hue. A large gash filled with dried blood crossed his cheek. Thomas dipped his father's handkerchief into a basin of water and dabbed at the crusty blood and dirt.

Thomas stepped back, saw his reflection again, and noticed the soldier's uniform collar on his neck for the first time. He fastened its brass buttons to the top. He reached behind him to gather up his queue. He wrapped it up and under the cap to make it fit.

"I *am* a soldier." Thomas straightened his shoulders and peered into the glass, past the ugly damage on his face. He brought the mirror in closer, his nose touching it. He looked deep into his eyes and searched for the Chinese that others saw and didn't like. He couldn't see it. Yes, there were his charcoal eyes, flat nose, and stark black hair, but Thomas saw only himself staring back at him—not a Chinese boy, just a regular boy: a Beck from Connecticut.

The men and boys assembled by company and stepped into dress parade. Thomas noticed the crowd forming—wagons and buggies parked in the worn grass, women in fine bonnets taking up under shade trees, their arms latched with their husbands. Young children shielded the sun with their hands, flushed faces mesmerized at the grand spectacle of the army.

Thomas's face reddened when he noticed a beautiful girl in yellow dress, her hair pinned up, a few strawberry-blonde strands falling loose and framing her heart-shaped face. She was thin and tall, with eyes that Thomas imagined sparkled when she smiled: green, with specks of gold from the sunlight, Thomas fancied. He knew her name was lovely, too, something akin to her beauty, like Julia or Michaela or Maria. She glanced his way. Thomas diverted his eyes and smiled sheepishly.

Oh, what I wouldn't give to spend time with a lassie like that!

The march moved past the girl and Thomas regretted it. He resisted the temptation to turn back and look, but allowed himself another grin. Funny how his body tingled at the sight of her. Thomas rather enjoyed it.

He carried on and noticed that the multitude also included Negroes, many in fact. They stood nearby the others, watching with eager eyes.

What must they think of us? Thomas wondered. *Do they feel hope when they see our troops? Are they aware the country's been torn apart over them? What would they think about a Chinese Yankee?*

Thomas locked eyes with a black man. Thomas knew he was staring, but he couldn't bring himself to look away. The man nodded to him and Thomas returned it. The man then offered him a slow salute, touching his forehead with two fingers. Thomas's stomach flip-flopped.

A bugler signaled halt, and the company stood like statues for the officers' review. The drumbeats and bugle songs stirred pride into Thomas's soldier heart—a heart that nearly pounded out of his chest as the colonel approached. The officer paused and gave Thomas the once-over. Thomas clenched his teeth and looked straight forward, avoiding eye contact.

When the colonel moved past, Thomas let his breath go, not

realizing he'd been holding it. Somehow and someway, Thomas had passed muster.

When the fife and drums of the regimental band fell silent, the boys moved out of line and dispersed into the gathered crowd. Thomas scanned the faces, hoping beyond reason to see his mama and pa, but knew his search was a fool's errand.

Joseph's ship was probably still out at sea and his mama rarely ventured beyond the homestead. Thomas recalled the news about the big train wreck at South Norwalk in 1853. The New York and New Haven Train had plunged into the river after its conductor missed a signal, the drawbridge having been raised for a steamer. Nearly ten years had passed, but Madeline still kept the *Hartford Courant* article folded in her Bible, a reminder of the dangers that lie beyond the farm. She brought it out whenever Thomas asked to accompany Robert to town.

Even if she had been willing, Thomas worried that his mama didn't have the means to depart the homestead. Thomas had shelled out a generous price to a Hartford blacksmith to get Barney home to her, but the surly man had regarded him suspiciously. Thomas hoped the money had appealed to his better nature.

Thomas weaved through the crowd, fought against a creeping loneliness, and looked again for the beautiful girl he'd seen on parade march. Then he made a sudden stop. His mama and pa stood a few feet away with Robert. Thomas's breath hitched when his mama embraced his brother.

Thomas couldn't move. His feet were like stone.

Will Robert want me there?

Thomas wrestled with what to do, watching as his pa shook Robert's hand. Joseph looked past Robert into the crowd as if searching for something. Then his eyes fell on Thomas. He motioned for him to come.

Thomas coerced his feet to move and took cautious steps forward.

"Hello, Pa."

"It does me good to see you, Thomas." Joseph took him by the shoulders. The elder Beck inspected Thomas's uniform, lifted his chin to see the gashes lining his face.

"Looks like the war found you early." His father's eyebrows rose, the truth he was surmising showing in his eyes.

"Just friendly war games, Pa." Joseph turned his head in the direction of loud conversation nearby—Henry and others from the company pointed fingers their way.

"War games, you say?" His father turned his attention back to Thomas. "Looks like you're the only one playing them."

"I'm keeping a clear head, Pa. Trying my darnedest, anyway."

"Aye, stay focused on what's ahead, like I always told you, my boy."

"I am, Pa, honest. Only I can't really see what's ahead for me. That boy over there," Thomas pointed at Henry, "he thought I was a slave. Pa, tell me about the Chinese coolie trade. Was I a slave in China?"

"You are my son." Joseph sniffed, waving his hand across his face. "The son I chose for myself."

Thomas wanted to protest, to inquire more about his life—or at least what life was like in China—before he ended up on his father's ship, but his pa's words muzzled his question.

"I'm fond of you, Pa."

"Aye, and me of you, my boy."

"Thomas." He relaxed into his mother's hug. She'd waited patiently with Robert while Joseph had hold of her other son. Thomas took a great deep breath as the ridicule, shame, and regret of enlisting, and getting beat, threatened to overtake his emotions.

"Mama, I'm so very sorry. Don't blame Robert. I promised him I'd return home and explain everything to you. I intended to, but—"

"But you had to stand up for what you believe in." His mother finished for him. "Your father and I raised you two to be good and honorable men. I just didn't expect it to happen so soon."

Thomas had barely opened his mouth to speak when the drum beats beckoned. Madeline pressed a piece of parchment into Thomas's palm, brought his hand up to her cheek, and kissed it. Wiping tears from her eyes, she pointed him toward his father.

Joseph put his arms around his sons' shoulders and walked with them to a borrowed wagon. The horse hitched to it wasn't Barney, but pa confirmed the old chestnut had made it back home.

"So long, Pa." Robert turned to Madeline and winked. "Mama, may God grant you safe journey on the tracks."

"He got me here to my sons. I reckon by his grace that he'll get me back home again, even if by an awful train." Robert had managed to coax a tender smile from his mama's lips even though she had misty eyes. Thomas thought it was nice to see his playful big brother again.

Madeline leaned forward and both boys kissed her on the cheek. Joseph helped her up into the wagon seat. An unwelcome thought passed through Thomas's mind.

What if this goodbye is the last goodbye?

He was a soldier after all, readying for his first battle. So was Robert.

"I'm not especially pleased that you both disobeyed your mother and enlisted," Joseph gathered his sons together, "but I am proud of you. I expect you to be brave, to fight with all you have, and," he looked straight at Robert. "I expect you to take care of each other. You are brothers."

"Yes, sir, Pa. Brothers," Robert repeated, his face turned down.

The exhausting soreness of the beating seemed heavier now as the wagon drove away. Madeline turned to wave and Thomas returned it with a flourish. If, God forbid, this was the last time she'd lay eyes on him, he wanted her memory to be a happy one.

"Jeremiah chapter one, verse five." Thomas clutched his mama's note. His mother was a persistent and determined woman and he loved her for it.

"The answers to all the country's problems can be found here," she had said once, giving her Bible a gentle thump. The same was true for Thomas, she asserted. Where her youngest son was concerned, the Book of Jeremiah was her treasure map, filled with lots of clues to help Thomas find his way.

"Before I formed thee in the belly I knew thee...." Thomas knew the verse by heart. Whenever he wondered about why he was different, Madeline recited God's words.

"God is like a painter. He conceived you and then he created you exactly as he planned. Who are you to question it?"

Thomas marveled at his mama's cleverness—a trait she shared with his pa. They both knew how to end a discussion before Thomas could get a word in edgewise.

With no cause to doubt his mama, or God for that matter, Thomas accepted that he was meant to be exactly who he was. But he did wonder why.

Why am I a Chinese Yankee? It would be easier to be just a plain and regular Yankee like the others.

Thomas shrugged, supposing that only time would tell.

The noise of soldiers breaking camp brought him out of his thoughts just as his pa steered the wagon around a corner and disappeared from view. Thomas hurried to his tent mates to see four white squares on the ground where their camp tent had once stood. Henry and James each grabbed one. Elias did the same and Thomas followed suit. He held the canvas in his hand—it felt like tent material, but it was slight, definitely not big enough for a man to sleep in. The drums sounded. He'd have to figure it out later.

When the company was ready, they departed Camp Foote and marched in columns of four into Hartford. They made their way to the Hartford-New York steamboat wharf located at the end of State Street. Crowds of spectators watched from both sides and some of the soldiers gave friendly waves on their way.

The Fourteenth Connecticut boarded a steamer ship, the *City of Hartford,* which would transport them, after stops in Middletown, Middle Haddam, and Elizabethport, New Jersey, to trains bound for Washington City.

Although standing in a sea of soldiers, Thomas felt alone on the deck. He was buoyed by his parents' visit, but missed them desperately and now more than ever. His beloved Connecticut, the only home he'd ever really known, slowly disappeared from his sight.

CHAPTER SIX

The steamer ship docked after two days. Thomas touched hard ground for a brief moment before being packed into an old cattle train. He hated the train car; smelly and hot bodies closed him in, the wooden crate memory returning.

Thomas couldn't see daylight except through the slats in the railcar's side. He knew they drew closer to the war with every advance of the train and that twisted his insides. Still, he was praying for the trip's quick end when screeching train wheels forced his eyes open. A huge light entered when the heavy door released. Thomas rushed to the breach, thirsty for fresh air.

Thomas's eager feet tangled with other disembarking soldiers, forcing him to fall into the street, hard and sudden. He pushed himself up with his arms, only to be pulled down again. Henry stood on his queue.

"Henry, get off." Thomas used his hand to grab his braid, tugging to remove it from under Henry's boot. A crowd formed. Henry added another foot.

"Oh, now what's the hurry, monkey boy?" Henry laughed, eager to please the gathering. "Ya know ya look like them monkeys I saw in the traveling zoo in Hartford? Small and smelly with long tails above their rear. They make funny noises, too— kinda like ya sound when ya talk."

Henry stepped from Thomas's queue and grabbed it with his hand.

"Lookee here," Henry beckoned. He lowered himself to all fours and bounced on his tiptoes and fingertips, pulling Thomas's braid near his backside as he hopped. "Monkeys don't walk so good. I guess the tail gets in the way."

Thomas winced from the sting of his hair being pulled, but the sting of his comrades' laughter hurt worse. A bugle blared and Henry let go.

"Best ya get back to scampering along there, Monkey."

Thomas brushed off the dirt, thankful the throng departed. Steeling himself against the humiliation, Thomas started in their direction.

His feet slowed when he caught sight of a gleaming white dome, only partially finished, but still strikingly beautiful. Thomas squinted into the sunlight to better see the marble Capitol Building. It was the largest, most remarkable structure he'd ever seen. How incredible to be in Washington City.

"The center of the US government is here." Thomas took in the view. "Well, maybe just for the Northern states—for now."

That's why I'm here, Thomas considered, *to help bring the country back together and free the slaves*. Abraham Lincoln wanted that; it's why the South left the Union in the first place. A thought sparked in Thomas's mind. *Abraham Lincoln is here, right here, and well, so am I. How grand!*

Thomas was filled with anxious and excited energy. People lined the streets—men in tall hats, women in fancy dresses and umbrellas to provide shade, black men carrying trunks and driving wagons. Children held their fathers' coattails or stood near their mamas, thumbs in their mouths. Wagon traffic moved in every direction on roads that intersected as far as the eye could see. Thomas wanted to see the White House. He bet Robert did, too, but Thomas couldn't spot him in the masses still exiting the trains.

When the time came for the regiment to march, Thomas got his wish. The Fourteenth traveled down Pennsylvania Avenue, passing by the president's home on their way to the Long Bridge, a mile-long wooden connection over the Potomac River that stretched from Washington, the capitol of the Union, to Virginia, the state that contained the Confederacy's capitol city of Richmond.

So this bridge—this river—is what separates the North from the South. The gravity of the conflict crystallized for Thomas as he made his way across the long platform. *This water separates slave from free.*

A soldier behind Thomas could be heard cursing and spitting into the dirt as they stepped from the bridge. As Thomas's own feet landed in what was now considered a foreign land, the soldier belted out a loud shout.

"We've entered the enemy's front yard, boys."

The Fourteenth Connecticut heard distant booms and crashes like cannon fire as they marched along the dusty dirt roads of the Virginia countryside. Majestic green mountains were in view as they went. With excitement for a battle building, the men and boys forgot to be exhausted from their three-day journey.

The regiment expected the sounds of war to pick up as they traipsed. They expected to feel the earth shake beneath their feet; they turned their ears to the ground for the *ping, ping* and *pop, pop* of musket fire. Instead, a low groan spread across the landscape, the winds whispering, not hammering.

The boys had hoped that their first march would end in a great and noble clash of armies, but the Fourteenth was headed to guard duty at Fort Ethan Allen. Their mission was to maintain the defenses of Washington after the Second Battle of Bull Run, which had ended in another Confederate victory.

The fact of protection detail infected the line like soldier's disease infected camp. But instead of being forced to spend hours in stomach distress, the boys felt heavy and tired, their pride-filled stomps seceding into slow, sloughing steps.

So much for meeting the elephant.

Orders came to fall out in a valley just off the dirt road. Henry tossed his sack into a tree. "First they file us onto a steamer ship and pack us in like fish caught in a net. Then, without any rest, they cram us onto a cattle car like a bunch of animals bound for the slaughter. Now we've had a nice fine walk, but there's no enemy, no battle—not even a skirmish. And nothing but a few crackers, a morsel of cheese, and a bit of ham to eat in three whole days...."

"Welcome to the army," James deadpanned.

"Had ourselves nice fine camp tents at home," Henry persisted, loosening the white square from his bundle. "Now what have we got?"

"We got this." James held up his canvas, let it unfold. The shape was a rectangle and it was outlined with circular grommets.

"What's this? Some kind of rigid blanket?"

"It's a two-man tent, ya imbecile," Henry groused. "See, yours attaches to mine."

"If you already knew that, why'd you ask me in the first place?"

Elias sorted through his things for his canteen and headed toward a tree line. Thomas, who had been watching the exchange between Henry and James, took a cautious step forward.

"Pardon me, Elias, may I accompany you?"

"Oh, hello, Thomas." Elias turned. "Yes, of course. I'm in search of some water."

The pair ambled for a time without speaking, eventually coming to a slow-running creek. Thomas fidgeted with the wide strap on his canteen.

"You like coffee?" he finally asked Elias, dipping his vessel into the water.

"Yep, I do." Elias crouched next to him. "I always drink it with my pa after supper."

"I never tried it until I joined up. It takes some getting used to."

"I reckon a lot of things take some getting used to in the army."

"Not just the army," Thomas mumbled.

"It's a strange thing—you're a strange thing, Thomas, if you don't mind me saying." Thomas didn't. At least it was the truth. "I can't say I've ever seen a Chinese person before. Never heard of China before neither."

"It's a long ways away. I barely remember it. Just snippets, like dreams, you know?" Thomas brought his braid around to rest on his shoulder.

"Do all Chinese wear their hair like that?"

"My father did and my uncle, too. My pa told me it was because of the emperor."

"Is that like a president, like Abe Lincoln?"

"I don't think so. My *baba* was taken from the fields by soldiers with swords. Hard to imagine that here. I'm afraid that's all I know."

"More isn't necessary." Elias filled his jug. "'Judge not, lest you be judged,' the Bible says."

"Wish the other boys felt that way." Thomas returned the lid of his canteen. "You don't speak much, Elias. Is there a reason for it?"

"Nah, no reason. Henry does enough talking for all of us, doesn't he?" Elias had a smile in his voice.

"Yes, I suppose he does." Jitters infected Thomas's gut. "Elias, um—"

"Yes, Thomas?"

"Well, you see, the shelter halves they gave us...would you want to share one, ah, with me?"

"I'd be honored."

Whoops and hollers filled the air around Thomas, the din thrilling, howls, and rousing yells. Men patted each other on the back and waved their caps. A heavy hand slapped Thomas's shoulder, a soldier celebrating the drums' cadence. Thomas joined in, raised his voice at the top of his lungs. After suffering through guard duty, which this time meant just standing around staring at a vast empty landscape, the boys rejoiced at the news of heading straight to the fight.

Thomas's raucous yells lightened his spirit, although his body remained stiff and sore from Henry's beating. His chest felt full; intoxicating swells burst in his chest. He'd never felt so alive.

Thomas needed Robert. He darted around as the company struck tents.

"Robert," he shouted at the top of his lungs. Thomas spun in a circle, shouting as he went. "Robert."

"Trying to wake the dead, are ya, Thomas?"

Thomas stopped mid-turn, almost stumbled to the ground.

"Robert. We're joining the fight. Gonna meet old General Lee."

Robert pulled Thomas behind his shelter tent, one of the few still standing. Away from watching eyes, Robert pulled his brother into a warm embrace.

"I know, Tom." Robert winked. "It's a coming—we're gonna get us some Rebs."

A broad smile escaped Thomas's lips. For the first time since they'd been mustered in, Thomas recognized the familiar twinkle in his brother's eyes. He hoped their father's words had sunk in—hoped Robert would be his brother again. The two boys fell in with their regiment.

CHAPTER SEVEN

For nine days the regiment marched through the most beautiful country Thomas had ever seen. The rolling hills and green and mustard fields seemed almost majestic as they passed, not that any of Thomas's fellow soldiers noticed. The boys plodded through the dusty paths with their heads down, many seeming to fall asleep to the rhythmic *left, right, left, right* of their footsteps, eyes closed to block the dirt their shoes kicked up.

The scenery drastically changed on the tenth day as they neared Sharpsburg, Maryland. Union troops streamed in from the opposite direction. Men dressed in white bandages, blood soaking through, plodded with heavy steps. Other men carried wounded comrades on litters. A lump rose in Thomas's throat and he swallowed down hard.

His regiment fell out to let ambulance wagons pass. Thomas flinched, the shrill groans making him shudder. He looked away from large lumps under blankets writhing in pain, but he couldn't stop their dreadful cries from reaching his ears.

After a prolonged wait for the wagons to make their way through, the company resumed the march. Whispers, prayers, and curses could be heard up and down the line, including Thomas's own.

"They've seen the elephant," Thomas muttered aloud with a new understanding of what going into battle really meant. Panic sped his heart-beats. He fought it, squeezing his eyes shut to squelch the scary sights. Thomas had been curious about his first battle, but now a terrible fear consumed him.

He yearned to find out what his brother thought. Thomas stretched his neck, searched for blond curls underneath caps ahead. Finally, he got a glimpse. Robert shook his head from side to side and his body twitched. Even from his backside, several rows of soldiers between them, Thomas recognized his brother's feelings.

"Fit to be tied," Thomas whispered. "Robert's got his dander up. Those Rebs better watch out."

The panic that gripped Thomas faded now as anger at the enemy filled him, too.

The boys shivered as their shoes sank into the deep and slippery waters of Antietam Creek, fording it as they moved toward the sounds of the battle. For two miles they marched with squishy steps until they reached a dense tree line.

The Fourteenth Connecticut reached the woods with the 108th Pennsylvania on its right and the 108th New York on its left. Thomas realized that their Second Brigade was like the ham in a sandwich. The Third Brigade was on top and in front; the First Brigade was bringing up the rear. Together they formed a line of battle.

"Load weapons." The order was shouted in unison by officers around them and came across surprisingly loud and clear.

Thomas obeyed with haste. He didn't know exactly what would come in the next few minutes, but he wanted powder in his musket. He worked to quell the images of the wounded and crying soldiers from rising in his mind, but he couldn't halt them. The Fourteenth Connecticut would soon attack the Rebels who were responsible for that. Would their regiment do the same kind of damage? Would it be done to them?

The Fourteenth passed by farm buildings as the Third Brigade came to a fence dividing a meadow from a cornfield. As they passed over it, shots and shells rang out, their position revealed to Confederate batteries.

Horrifying sounds of booming cannons reached Thomas's ears, like all of Hartford's Fourth of July fireworks were erupting during a thunderstorm. He clamped down his cap with his left hand, his head turned to the ground as they went, fighting the urge to run. A cannon ball streaked by so close that he felt a whoosh of air around his ear, the scream of it ending with an explosion nearby, taking the leg off a comrade. Smoke filled the air and dirt rained down on him.

Panic seized Thomas. He screamed but couldn't hear his own voice. His body felt sick and heavy. He froze in place.

"C'mon Chinaman, get moving," a soldier shouted. "You make a better target standing still, yellow boy."

Thomas felt pressure on his back, the force of the entire regiment making him go, the *left, right* of his training taking over his feet.

When the Fourteenth reached the fence, the boys clambered up and over with sweat heavy on their brows. He watched the Third Brigade ascend a hill; their goal was the ridge ahead where smoke rose from concealed guns.

Actual soldiers are up there, Thomas marveled. *The enemy is there, right in front of us. These men are as mad as us. Their weapons are pointed at...me.*

This battle had real soldiers, real bullets, and real...death. Thomas's spine went straight. He shook his head and spat to deny the nervousness that enveloped him. He grabbed his queue and tucked it into his coat, a reminder of how far he'd come to be here on this day. This was it—Thomas's chance to prove that a Chinese Yankee could fight as well as a regular one. No matter how frightened, Thomas intended to meet the battle head-on.

The army in front of him waged war to keep their way of life, a way that depended on enslaving people. Thomas couldn't grasp all the newspaper talk about commerce or exactly why cotton was king in the South, but he remembered the Negro man who saluted him at the review. That gentleman needed Thomas.

And if people—even some in the North—can look at me and see a slave, well, all the more reason for me to fight against actual slavery. I have to do my duty. There are some who don't think I should be allowed to fight, and the enemy out there wants me dead.

"I get to fight now," Thomas said, clutching his musket as the Fourteenth climbed the rise.

The screams were loud and terrifying. The men in front of Thomas had reached the crest of the hill and were met with a horrible volley of Minie balls, the Rebels waiting for them in a sunken road, their rifles cocked and ready.

The Confederate fire downed the Union line in a rapid fashion, dominoes falling at once and together. Those who did not fall in those dreadful minutes made a swift retreat, sprinting back through their lines and away from the heat of the muskets.

The men of the Fourteenth Connecticut strained to maintain formation, but the wave of the shell-shocked regiments was too strong and the line began to break. A Union colonel raised his saber to rally his men—and to divert their attention away from the fleeing men whose eyes were wild with fear.

Thomas's approach stalled in the smoke and confusion. A wounded soldier with a hole in his chest stumbled toward him and fell, knocking both of them from their feet. Thomas ate dusty dirt as they hit the ground hard. Trapped beneath the soldier's heavy body, Thomas strained to push him off.

Once freed, Thomas reached out, wishing to help, but the soldier was dead. He rose to stand, but staggered, a sickening feeling incasing him. His pulse quickened as he remembered his brother.

"Robert."

Thomas sprang up and scanned the line to his right, looking for him. He forgot the battle. Shots whizzed past, soldiers fell near him. The battle moved around his head and Thomas felt dizzy from the smoke and noise and noxious fumes of gunpowder. Where was Robert? Thomas needed to know—now.

Thomas moved through the line and searched the blue uniforms. He should be close, Thomas reasoned, their advancing line closing ranks to fill gaps left by the killed and wounded. Thomas ran straight into his sergeant.

"Oh, now boy-o, where ya headed?" The stout man pointed out to the rise in front of them. "The enemy is up that a ways. Or are ya yellow like your skin?"

"But my brother." Thomas forgot his protocol when speaking to a higher rank.

"Um, sorry, Sarge," Robert interjected in a loud voice, reaching their position. "This boy got lost. I'll watch out for him."

Thomas raised his head to the heavens and offered a quick 'thank you' as Robert pulled him to his side.

"Let's go, Tom," Robert shouted. "Let's get these Rebs together."

Step by hastened step, the brothers climbed the hill with their company. Thomas struggled to match the stride and speed of his much taller brother. He grunted and sweltered his way up, the anticipation choking him as much as the dense fog of battle.

They reached the top of the small incline and straightaway understood why the survivors from the Third Brigade had fled. Their path emptied into a road that sat lower than the surrounding farmland, a perfect place for the Rebels to bide their time until the next wave of blue came—and they were the next wave.

Thomas and Robert sighted their weapons mid-stride. Thomas's finger nearly slipped off the trigger, but he gripped it harder as an icy cold sliced through his chest. He fired his weapon at a mass of gray with his eyes wide open.

"Keep coming," a lieutenant shouted. "Keep the fire hot, boys. Keep shooting."

Thomas kneeled down beside a young corporal, the man's eyes wide open but unseeing. He concentrated on reloading as shots whistled past him. Robert, to his right, was also reloading. Thomas fretted about how long the process was taking as he and Robert were exposed in front. The fire grew hot around them, more boys falling in heavy thumps and awful shrieks. There was no way forward except down into the lane of armed Rebels. There was no way for the brothers to maintain their position and avoid a bullet.

Orders bellowed out, forcing the Fourteenth to retreat and make way for more blue troops to advance for their turn at the sunken road. The regiment stepped backwards, a dangerous descent down the hill, but they loaded and fired during the retreat. Thomas mimicked the actions of the regiment. It helped him to resist the urge to turn and run straight back down the hill.

The Fourteenth finally gathered in an adjacent cornfield, where they continued to shoot with mechanical fury in support of the other ascending blue troops.

For three long hours, Union and Confederate troops contested that sunken lane intersecting the two Maryland farms owned by the Mumma and Roulette families. While in the thick of the fight, Thomas had noted the advancing blue waves, one after another. He prayed that the Fourteenth had paved the way, that the regiments who attacked after them would finally drive the gray troops out.

When the firing had ceased, the regiment assembled and overlooked the sunken road. It was littered with the bodies of hundreds of Confederate soldiers.

"Look at them." James stared down into the pit. "What a bloody mess."

"I heard them call it Bloody Lane," Henry added. "That'll teach them to mess with us. This will send old General Lee back where he belongs."

"Hope they get them buried before the stink reaches us up here."

Thomas's gut turned over. He ran to a nearby ditch and vomited. His tears pooled as he swallowed down the acrid taste of his own puke. Exhaustion overwhelmed him and he lay there on the hard ground, unable to move. He fell into a deep sleep.

CHAPTER EIGHT

The boys in blue found a new energy on the march, relieved to put distance between themselves and the bloody battle. It was behind them now—the desperate screams of the wounded, the rotted meat smell of dying horses and men, and the mix of sweat, ash, and smoke that clung to the soldiers' uniforms.

As the Fourteenth Connecticut passed by other regiments, the tired soldiers nevertheless wore their battered uniforms with pride. They could no longer be called green recruits. Despite the dirt and the grime, the battle-tested *veterans* had a spring in their steps that any passing onlooker would surely note.

Their Army of the Potomac had stopped General Lee's advance, and even though the price of victory had been high, the boys knew that the newspapers at home would soon write about their first engagement being a winning one.

Thomas stepped in tune with the others and felt a deep connection with the Fourteenth and the big army of which they were a part. Thomas, the Chinese Yankee, had gotten his chance to fight with them—with Robert—just as he'd always hoped. And even though there was an uneasy and uncomfortable wrenching in his gut about so many Union and Confederate dead, there was also a strange peace that made its home in Thomas's heart from simply being a part of it.

His first battle had been exhilarating and exhausting, frightening and satisfying. Thomas doubted that anyone could really describe the entirety of what it was like, but for him, it was enough that they were all feeling it together. It meant everything to Thomas to take part—to be a part—of something as big and monumental as the battle of Antietam. It wasn't lost on Thomas that he once had feared never getting this chance. Thomas's steps may have been the springiest of all.

The Fourteenth Connecticut arrived at Bolivar Heights near Harper's Ferry, Virginia, several days later. Brought together by the call of assembly, soldiers gathered to hear a general order issued by the president. Curiosity reigned. Surely the war wasn't over—old Bobby Lee would reassemble and try again—but what news gathered them?

Thomas jockeyed for a place close to the general. Using his small size to his advantage, he weaved in between his bigger comrades and positioned himself close enough to hear.

"That on the first day of January, in the year of our Lord one thousand eight hundred and sixty-three, all persons held as slaves within any state or designated part of a state, the people whereof shall then be in rebellion against the United States, shall be then, thenceforward, and forever free...."

Free? Thomas gulped. *President Lincoln is freeing the slaves?* All kinds of noise came from the troops and the call sounded for attention.

"...And the executive government of the United States, including the military and naval authority thereof, will recognize and maintain the freedom of such persons, and will do no act or acts to repress such persons, or any of them, in any efforts they may make for their actual freedom."

Thomas stretched his neck to hear more.

"...And I further declare and make known, that such persons of suitable condition will be received into the armed service of the United States..."

After the general read the entire order, the regiment fell out.

"I didn't sign up to free no darkies." Henry built up the fire, as the boys huddled together in camp.

"What's it matter, Henry?" James ran a hand down the length of his beard. "There ain't no slaves in Connecticut anyway. All it's gonna do is make the South fighting mad—not like they needed another reason to fight."

"Why shouldn't they be free?" Elias chimed in. "The war started because folks didn't want slavery expanding—why not get rid of it all together?"

"Your papa, the preacher, he's one of them...what do you call them? Abolitionists?" Henry grimaced. "The ones who want freedom for the slaves?"

"Yes, he is," Elias retorted. "He is good friends with the Beecher family; says the Bible teaches us about the dignity of all people. God delivered slaves out of Egypt—"

"Them slaves weren't darkies! You saying black folks deserve rights? You wanna work alongside them, sit by them in church?"

Henry glared at Thomas. "You want them joining our army like China boy here? This ain't their country; it's ours."

"That Beecher woman—Harriett—she done started this whole thing with that book of hers—*Uncle Tom's Cabin* or whatever it's called."

"She merely told the truth about slavery, James," Elias responded.

"I've heard enough," Thomas pronounced. He stepped around the fire, the familiar sorrow infecting him. He pulled the tent flap open and disappeared inside.

Thomas took parchment out from under his bed roll to start a letter, but words failed him. Thoughts jumbled and swirled in his head, causing it to ache. Thomas groaned, willed the anger and sadness to depart.

No use. He *was* angry. Fitting in and taking part were all he wanted—a chance to fight for his country like his brother.

But it's not my country, Thomas thought, *at least not according to them.*

Thomas crumpled the paper, grabbed another one, and shredded it. He couldn't say these things to his mama. He'd prove her right. Outside, the conversation grew more intense. Henry's voice rose above the others.

"Slaves are slaves for a reason. They're no better than dogs. They don't have any rights."

"Well, that's not what Mr. Lincoln thinks, Henry," Elias disagreed. "You best get behind it."

Thomas took another deep breath. He encountered Henry's everywhere in camp. Thomas wore the same uniform as them and fought alongside them, but he wasn't one of them. Even the soldiers who refrained from calling him names refused him a passing smile. No one shared their coffee beans or offered him their canteen. No one stood next to him during church services unless there was no other space to fill.

Robert withheld his time, too. While Thomas felt grateful for his brother's friendliness in their private moments, it still left him wanting. Thomas longed for their idle times in camp to be spent together doing the things they did on the farm—playing cards, searching for treasures in the woods, mapping out pretend battle plans—but Robert had a different notion. Whenever Thomas got a glimpse of him, he was doing those things with Fred and William, who hadn't been welcoming to Thomas. Robert's rejection hurt the most.

"My own brother," Thomas whispered.

Thomas considered the president's proclamation, recalled Ms. Stowe's book, when the slave, George Harris, laments to his wife,

Eliza, about his bondage.

"My life is bitter as wormwood; the very life is burning out of me. I'm a poor, miserable forlorn drudge...what's the use of our trying to do anything, trying to know anything, trying to be anything? What's the use of living? I wish I was dead!"

The questions pinged through Thomas's head. Some things did seem hopeless—war certainly did. Many men and boys died at Antietam—some maybe because Thomas had fired his musket. The thought made him ill. How terrible a soldier's duty.

Thomas rubbed his temples. Since war was a horrible thing—and Antietam had proven that—then there needed to be a very good—a just—reason for waging it. Maybe preserving the union as one country wasn't enough, but ending slavery had to be. Henry's voice wafted through the tent.

"Yes, what's the use?" Thomas echoed the words aloud.

The North could lose the war. *And what if we win? Will these boys like me any more than they do now? Probably not if their reaction to the president's decree is any hint. If they have to accept me—and all the slaves once free—they'll probably like me less.*

Thomas didn't know any black folk personally, but his father had spoken of the kind and respectful men who delivered supplies to him on the wharf, about strong and able dock workers. Joseph

Beck treated honest men fairly; their being a Negro didn't matter. Because of his father's example, Thomas would refuse to judge a man until he knew the man.

"Doesn't stop Henry, does it?" Thomas voiced his question.

Maybe Thomas didn't want to be one of the boys after all, at least not like Henry. He wrung his hands and wished the struggle would disappear like a nightmare with the rising sun.

Stretching out, Thomas considered why he joined the army. He hadn't been driven by adventure, not fully. He had wanted the opportunity to make his own life away from the Beck homestead and do his part to stop the spread of slavery.

I want to be an American and live an American life. If President Lincoln wants to give the slaves a chance to do that, well then, so be it.

CHAPTER NINE

My dearest Mama,

Forgive me the tardiness of my letter. I'm sure you read in the Courant about the great battle of Antietam Creek, near a town called Sharpsburg in Maryland, in September. It made things mighty confusing for the post rider for a time, trying to track down our troops. Mama, Robert and I came out of it unscathed. Praise be. Please tell Pa that we gave battle alongside each other. He will be happy to hear it.

I overheard the boys say the papers called the battle a great Northern victory. Having been there, I can say that it was, at best, a draw, with many dead on both sides. Battle is so loud, Mama. The cannon fire and musket shots thunder in your ears so strong that you can't think. All you can do is fire at the enemy because they are shooting at you. A boy who was shot fell into me—I didn't know him—and he died as I lay beside him. It shocked me something awful. I worry, too, that maybe my gun killed some Rebels along the way. Mama, what does the Bible say about killing when it's your duty?

You must be relieved that President Lincoln is freeing the slaves. I certainly am, but a lot of the boys here disagree. They seem angrier at me than usual, but I still don't understand why. I only want to help them win the war. Just so you don't fret, they haven't laid hands on me again, Mama. My body has healed. They don't like me much, but on the march, a boy named Elias—he's eighteen, too, like Robert—shared a tent with me. You would like him. He carries the Bible with him and knows it almost as well as you.

I hear the bugler now and so must go. The army is camped now at Falmouth, Virginia. We were told to erect a log hut to keep us warm now that it's November. Please write soon. I send my deepest affections to you and Pa.

Your son,

Thomas

A beautiful sunrise flooded the landscape with soft light and blanketed it with color. Fallen leaves left a blanket of gold and deep red on the camp floor. Thomas drew in the air. The smoking cook fires reached his flat nose—the delicious scents of wood and sizzling bacon set off pangs of hunger.

Thomas sipped coffee from a tin cup as he approached the site where his bunkmates determined to build their winter shelter.

"Hey, James. Grab that log there and affix it here, sideways," Henry shouted.

A carpenter back home in Connecticut, Henry led their group's efforts to build their hut. He picked a good spot, on a slight rise. Makeshift structures were erected on both sides, but Henry's looked sturdier. For the first time, Thomas was glad to be his bunkmate.

As he watched the boys build, it occurred to Thomas that Henry might not let him inside. The old army-issued camp tent was one thing, but a "house" built by Henry's own hands?

"May I be of assistance?" Thomas did his best to look aloof and unworried about Henry's answer.

"Go and dig our latrine, down the slope of the hill, behind our hut, China boy. That's how you can help."

"Yes, sir." Thomas made a fake salute in Henry's direction. Henry snickered.

Another latrine. That's just about the last thing I want to do right now. But if that's what they'll let me contribute, it'll be the best dang hole in the ground they have ever seen. And if it means I can sleep indoors, well, I'll dig all the way to China. Henry did say "our" hut, right?

Thomas chipped at the hard ground with his shovel, sluggish work, and finally dug a sufficient crater. His shoulder begging for relief, he watched the others gather logs and alternate them sideways, stacking them into log walls.

Henry, James, and Elias were nearly finished when Thomas completed his work. Henry designed the hut around the base of a tree, its top branches forming a Y that poked up from the center. The trio attempted to spread their tent canvas over the hut's top as a temporary roof.

"Darn it, Elias. Don't tear it. We won't stay dry if you rip the roof to shreds."

"I can't get up there, Henry. My foot keeps slipping." Elias was panting. "James, come round this side and grab it."

Thomas sprinted to them, entered the hut, and scurried up the tree. Soon he was at the Y, looking down at his bunkmates.

"Whoa, monkey-boy. Ya really are a monkey." Henry chuckled.

"You looked like you needed a hand."

Thomas untangled the tent from the Y branches, freeing the material so James and Elias could secure it to the other side of the shelter with rope threaded through the grommets and between the logs.

"Thank you, Thomas." Elias patted him on the back as Thomas slid down. "See, Henry? Thomas helped us out there."

"Darn right, Elias," James cackled. "Big ole Henry had gotten up there we would've had another casualty in the company—he would've fallen right through. That tree ain't big enough to handle that mass."

Thomas's breath caught in his throat. *Oh no, don't make Henry mad, not now.*

"Well, that's why the monkey's still around, right, Tommy?"

Thomas's head jerked up. Had Henry called him something other than China boy?

Just then, Robert passed by and beamed a bright smile.

"Hello, brother." Thomas smiled back.

Robert ambled with his friends, William and Fred, and several other boys. Thomas's smile retreated when he overheard their conversation.

"Having him for a brother, you might as well have a darkie for a mama," Fred opined. Robert glanced toward Thomas and then quickly back to Fred.

"Just shut up," Robert said. "Ya don't know anything."

"All these years hearing about your brother—and you ain't never said he was a Chinaman. I reckon you must agree with me."

Robert shoved Fred to the ground. Fred shot up and lunged toward Robert, but William and the others restrained him.

"Just calm down there, boys," another said.

Robert spat and walked away.

For the first time, Thomas realized he wasn't the only one struggling.

Buoyed by hearing Henry call him by name, Thomas sat down by the fire blazing in front of their new winter home. He figured on waiting forever to be invited to join the nightly gathering but didn't want to push his luck by asking for permission outright. So Thomas just sat. Since other soldiers from nearby huts also joined the group this night, he hoped to go unnoticed.

The boys talked about their girls back home or the first thing they wanted to eat when the war ended, dry biscuits, bacon grease, and watery coffee leaving them hungry for home cooking. Thomas longed to join the conversation—he'd say he missed fresh strawberries the most—but feared rejection, or worse, retaliation. He couldn't risk that.

Thomas rubbed his hands, blew into them. It had felt good to hear Henry call him Tommy. But it didn't last, the feeling replaced with sadness for his brother. Thomas couldn't find any peace that lasted beyond the battlefield or a fleeting moment.

"So, what's your story, Tommy?"

"I, um, came over on my father's ship." Thomas recovered from the shock of Henry's question. "He found me hiding as he sailed away from China on his way back to America."

"You remember how you got there?" Elias's blue eyes were friendly.

"A little," Thomas acknowledged. "My uncle said it was a good ship, stowed me there, said it would take me away and keep me safe."

"Safe from what?" Henry interrupted.

Thomas paused, not sure what to say next. The truth wouldn't help. Joseph told him that other countries were at the port in Kuangchou to collect coolies—Chinese indentured servants—not much better than slaves. Joseph had assumed that whomever placed Thomas on his ship was trying to save him from a coolie contract.

"I don't know all the details," Thomas finally said, which was true. "I was only six years old, or so my father guessed. He brought me home and raised me."

"Wait," James interjected. "You don't know how old you are?"

"I, well...I was *over* eighteen when I enlisted—"

"There ain't no officers here," James reminded him. "How old are you really?"

"The truth is I am not sure," Thomas confessed. "My father assumed I was about six when he found me, but my mama figured younger being as I was really small. I couldn't speak English. I've been with them for ten years so that makes fifteen or sixteen a good guess."

"As small ya are, I'm figuring more like twelve," Henry teased. "Don't make sense to me anyways. Why would your pa bring a Chinese boy into his house like family? Slave makes more sense.

How come he wasn't worried about what people would say?"

There was that ugly word again with its even uglier meaning. Thomas felt a ball of fury rounding up inside and a profound sadness, too, at knowing friendship with Henry—with these men—was still far beyond his grasp.

"Slavery is outlawed in the North, Henry, and you know that." Elias was quick to respond. "Thomas, you've had quite a time of it."

"My father has never cared for other people's opinions." Thomas's pride for his father rose above his swirling emotions. "He started calling me 'son' and named me Thomas after his own father."

"My home and family are in Connecticut," he continued. "Mama taught me how to read and write and do arithmetic with Robert's lessons from the schoolhouse."

"You didn't go to school?" James lowered his pipe.

Thomas said no, he hadn't. His mama hadn't wanted him to leave the farm.

"See?" Henry erupted. "They *were* ashamed of their slave son."

Henry rose and engaged a gaggle in a dice tossing card game down the lane. James finished his pipe and crossed into the log hut. Only Elias and Thomas remained. Thomas's shoulders shrunk and he crinkled away the tickle in his nose.

"Thank you for staying, Elias."

"No need." Elias brushed strands of long thin hair out of his eyes. "I think it's interesting, that's all."

"Which part?"

"How you can fight for the North, for our country, when folks like Henry are everywhere, thinking you can't fight, thinking you don't belong here."

Thomas thought a moment, chipped a twig into the fire. "I'm fighting to prove people like him wrong."

CHAPTER TEN

Some boys moaned and groaned when their turn came to man the pickets, but not Thomas. Even though the armies were holed up for the winter in their respective camps, he relished the opportunity to stand guard. Unlike digging trenches or building earthworks, this assignment got him out of camp and put his weapon back in his hand. It made Thomas feel useful.

"Thomas." Robert drew near.

"Hi ya, soldier." Thomas made a show of bowing before him, sweeping his cap to the ground flamboyantly. "You draw the short stick for guard duty, too?"

"I presume your winter quarters are sufficient? It sure seems so, seeing that you have the biggest hut in the company."

"You jealous, brother?"

"Just glad they let you in," Robert said, serious.

"Robert, I'm sorry for the other day, those boys—"

"Nothing ya need to apologize for." Robert bumped his brother's head affectionately.

"It's my fault the boys treat you that way," Thomas argued. "You wanted to come here and fight the South—not your friends."

"They're a bunch of blowhards." Robert kicked the ground. "Thomas, I'm not one for thinking too much on things...."

A crack snapped in the woods. Both boys' heads turned.

"Ya hear that Tom?"

"The Rebs wouldn't be this far forward, would they?" Thomas motioned in the direction of the sound. "How close are we camped to Lee's army?"

"Not that close. I reckon we ought to check it out, though, to be sure."

Robert took one ginger step, listened for any racket, and took another. Thomas traced Robert's footfalls.

"I've got an uneasy feeling." Robert turned back to his brother. "Ain't nowhere for us to hide among these bare trees."

"The Rebs can't hide either," Thomas pointed out.

The boys plodded forward, mouse-like, then another crack. Thomas's head veered that direction. He focused in through the woods and saw a shape lumbering through the naked tree trunks.

Thomas grabbed his brother's overcoat from behind, forcing him to stop. The boys crouched low. Thomas pointed out a man ahead of them about twenty yards away, his face turned down, a dirty gray hat popping into and out of the boys' view as he navigated over the forest floor.

"Is it a Reb?" Thomas whispered.

"Probably injured," Robert nodded. "He's moving mighty slow. Let's get closer."

The boys crept forward, their muskets pointed at the intruder. The boys watched the man sink into a little hill to rest.

"Halt there, Rebel." Robert ran to the man, his rifle pointed at him.

The boys pulled up short when the man's head turned up. The boys looked at each other with wide eyes, then back at the black man. His eyes displayed little fear, and he made no attempt to move. He bled from his side, his hand covered in a sticky goo. The back of his shirt was tattered into narrow strips, edged with a thick maroon substance that Thomas knew to be dried blood.

"Whipping gashes," Robert stated.

Thomas felt faint. He reached out for a nearby branch to steady himself.

Who is this man? Why is he out here in the woods? Is he a runaway?

Thomas shook the cobwebs from his head.

"He needs help."

"Mister? Are you alright?" Robert knelt down.

Humming a tune, the man didn't respond. His eyes didn't seem to register the boys' presence. Robert reached for the man's arm and the man recoiled.

"Easy," Robert said. "We can help ya."

Thomas ached to reassure the man, but fear held his voice. He'd never seen a black person up close. Thomas noted his wild, coarse, gray-tinged black hair under the hat, his thick lips and strong jaw. His sad mumbled song was chant-like, melodious. Thomas thought it could bespeak great joy, if not for the sorrowful moan in the man's throat.

Thomas closed his eyes to think. He felt a twinge from his queue pulling away from his head. Some strands had come loose and gotten caught up on his jacket button. As Thomas untangled and replaced the strands, it occurred to him that he probably looked as strange to this man as this man did to him.

Reaching down into his pocket, he grabbed a piece of hard tack and offered it to the man. If he was a runaway—and Thomas figured he had to be—he was probably hungry. Again, the man did not react, but his sing-song tune grew louder and stronger as if he was filled with the Spirit. The music reverberated off the tree limbs and Thomas got shivers down his spine.

Not content to return the dry biscuit to his pocket, Thomas reached for the man's free hand—the one not soaked in blood— and placed the biscuit in his open palm. The man felt it immediately and gazed down on it. He licked his lips once, twice, and brought it to his mouth. He ate it in a way that soldiers never did—with fervor and gratitude.

The two locked eyes and the man smiled at Thomas. At the sight of the man's glistening eyes, Thomas couldn't help but smile back.

Thomas's muscles strained under the massive weight of the man's body. He was really big and strong. It took all Thomas had to keep his footing and travel with the extra load. The man's blood soaked his uniform coat.

"Just a little farther, Tom," Robert grunted. "I see the medical tent."

Thomas's arm was latched with his brother's, the big man between them. The pair dragged him slowly as he was too exhausted or hurt to walk. A crowd encircled them.

"Why lookee what the cat dragged in," Henry called out. "That's the biggest rat I've ever seen. Looks like the cat got him good."

"Please let us pass," Thomas panted, his words labored in the cool air. "This man needs the doctor."

"Where did ya find him—and why didn't ya leave him out there with the other rats?" Soldiers from all over grew near, their questions coming like enfilade fire spraying all over the brothers.

"We found him while on pickets," Robert answered them, "and we're taking him to the medical tent. Now, please stand clear."

There were no attempts to move. Thomas's pulse quickened a bit. What would they do if the crowd charged them, if they tried to hurt this man?

"This ain't no slave state. Take him back." Thomas recognized the voice—it was Robert's friend William this time.

"William, by God, move!" Robert's voice struck a deep chord. "And God help ya if ya don't."

Robert lunged and took a big step forward. Thomas followed his lead. His brother was clearly done talking. It took all they had, but they pushed through, step by step, the man's legs dragging behind them. The crowd's rancor and loud voices didn't shrink away, but they dissipated enough that the Beck boys finally made it to the tent. They entered and gently dropped the man down onto a cot.

"Forgive us the intrusion, sir," Robert said to the surgeon. "This man could use your skills."

"Whew." Thomas wiped sweat from his brow and took a seat on a rock, relieved to be back at the pickets. Robert sat down on the cold, hard ground across from him. "I never expected that."

"Me neither. He must've been running away from his master, out looking for our troops or some way up to the free states in the North. I heard tale about some black folk attaching to the army, feeling safe from their masters behind our lines."

"His lashes—," Thomas stopped. "I've never seen anything so...cruel." He removed his cap and flung it.

"What are you thinking of?"

"That I'm a Tom-fool." Thomas scrunched his face. "When Henry calls me a slave, I feel injured, like I understand what they go through. I've got no right. I've never been owned by another man or felt the lashes of a whip."

"You mighta been, Tom, if pa hadn't found ya."

"Pa and mama gave me a good life, and now I'm a soldier. At least I have a chance to do something—not like him."

"President Lincoln's giving him a chance now," Robert reminded him. "And ya do understand him, maybe better than any of us can. Ya weren't whipped by a master's hand, but your row with Henry sure wasn't over a girl or a game of cards. I'm the foolhardy one."

"What makes you say that, Robert?"

"The way I figure it, we're out here fighting for our country—even fighting for black folks who are forced to be slaves. If we can do that, I sure as heck should be fighting harder on account of ya."

"What do you mean, Robert?" His brother's words surprised him.

"Don't know for sure. But you're out here risking your life, standing in harm's way, shooting the Secesh, same as everybody else in this regiment."

"I know."

"Maybe it will show them that you're an American, too. Maybe it even makes ya a better one, fighting for them when they treat ya that way."

Robert voiced everything Thomas had been thinking about but couldn't say. It hit him hard.

"I owe ya an apology, Tom."

"Never, Robert. You're fighting my battle with me. No one else will."

"Better late than never."

CHAPTER ELEVEN

The Fourteenth's notion of staying put for the winter proved incorrect. The Army of the Potomac resumed the march in December with the objective to capture the Confederate capitol of Richmond, Virginia. This time, instead of cheerful landscapes and the glow of autumn's sunshine on the soft, dusty earth, the troops trudged across cold, frozen roads, snowflakes pestering their faces, the fog of their breath rising to the gray skies above.

The Fourteenth Connecticut made its approach to Fredericksburg, Virginia. Regiment after regiment of Yankee troops neared the Rappahannock River in an impressive wave of blue. The march ended in a log jam of troops who were forced to wait their turn to cross over a 400-foot-wide section of icy, swollen water on pontoon bridges assembled by army engineers.

Thomas surveyed the scene: hundreds—no thousands—of Yankee soldiers, sparkling bayonets held high, marching in formation with their steps in tune. Regret flushed through Thomas. He couldn't see a path to victory for Lee's army with this many enemy troops headed their way. He almost felt sorry for them.

Thomas steeled himself against the harsh wind sweeping up from the frigid river as he approached the bridge. Moans and curses traveled down the line as the husky soldiers of the Fourteenth Connecticut left the security of the hard ground and stepped onto the wobbly pontoons. Thomas got a kick out of that. He didn't mind being on the water—it felt like home.

"*Děngdài!*" Thomas had shouted at Joseph, his little legs struggling to keep up with the big man working his way to the boat's stern. Thomas started after him, but the boat took a sharp rise and fall, knocking the boy to his knees. Joseph turned and hoisted Thomas up, carried him the rest of the way.

"Backstays."

Joseph pointed to the long lines that stretched from the stern to the tallest poles Thomas had ever seen up close. He followed Joseph's gaze upward, felt a little woozy and turned his head down to look into Joseph's friendly eyes.

"Mast," Joseph said.

"Mast," Thomas repeated.

"That-a-way, boy." A warm, enthusiastic smile spread onto Joseph's face. "You're getting it."

Thomas touched the stubble on Joseph's cheek, rested his head on Joseph's broad shoulder. Thomas tracked the Connecticut sailor this way for two months, learning English by repeating words like *bow*, *gaff*, *stern*, and his favorite, *compass*.

At bed down time, Joseph had tucked Thomas in his own cot, covered him with a blanket, and held his hand in prayer. Then the big man sprawled across the wood cabin floor, tucked his arms behind his head, and fell asleep. Thomas felt safe and warm, Joseph's snores accompanying the tossing of the ship, creating the perfect lullaby.

The Fourteenth Connecticut filed through Fredericksburg on

the twelfth day of the month. The town was deserted, the people having fled in panic at the sight of the Yankee troops. Under bombardment from Confederate shells trying to stop the Federal advance, the people took only the possessions they could carry along with them.

Thomas observed the cannon's devastating and effective work on stores and wrecked buildings. He got a chill when he realized that Fredericksburg was now a city populated by Northern soldiers. His Union army had occupied a Southern city—a good strategy for an army—but they had displaced thousands of innocent families in the process. It didn't seem to Thomas like something an army fighting for the freedom of others would do.

At nightfall, the men of the Fourteenth Connecticut sheltered in abandoned houses. Thomas followed Robert into a cellar and urged Elias to tag along with an overhand motion of his arm. Robert unearthed a candle and popped the lid on a jar of abandoned berry preserves. He scooped out a glob-full with his finger and passed it to Elias.

"Mighty delicious, if you ask me." Elias licked his finger and went in for another scoop.

"It was quite fine of the good folks of Fredericksburg to quarter and feed our tired troops, don't ya agree, Tom?" Robert had a joke in his voice. He handed the jar to Thomas, who motioned it away with his hand.

"What's itching ya?" Robert noted the far-off look in his brother's eyes.

"It doesn't feel right." Thomas reconsidered his decline of the jam as Elias licked his lips again. "I bet the Rebs aren't worried that we took the town. When has General Lee ever retreated? I bet they're dug in on those hills, lying in wait."

Dread filled the musty room. Elias swallowed down hard. Thomas regretted voicing his thoughts.

"Yep, you're probably right, Tom," Robert sliced through the uncomfortable silence, "but we'll lick 'em. There's so many of us. And," he motioned to the jar Elias held, "there's no use letting this jam go to waste."

CHAPTER TWELVE

The awful shelling between the armies resumed the next morning, the Fourteenth Connecticut finding cover behind the houses where they'd passed the night. Men huddled together, their lips moving, but Thomas couldn't hear their words. The air filled with the shrill whine of cannonballs and cascading booms as they exploded into nearby buildings. Debris flew everywhere.

"We're in a death trap!" Thomas exclaimed.

He bounced on his toes, anxious energy, and itched to get up the hill. Thomas had a good vantage point for watching blue troops march up a steep rise called Marye's Heights. They maintained good formation until disappearing slightly into a low depression and emerging moments later in front of a stone wall.

The Rebs poured lead into the Northern boys ascending the

hill. Entire lines of blue were swept aside in an instant. The fog from the guns briefly hid the horror, but then Thomas beheld a miracle, one after another. The blue troops re-formed, closed up, and kept moving forward.

"That's it, boys," Thomas screamed. "Keep at 'em. Let me at them."

Thomas's chest pounded and the bounce in his legs intensified. He wanted his turn up that slope. The Fourteenth Connecticut would break through!

Finally a sergeant motioned for them to form a line. Thomas shot to the front. He strode with determined steps up the snow-dusted incline, fear gripping him as bullets flew down like sheeting rain. Fighting the rising sickness in his chest, Thomas pressed on, his bayonet forward, loading and shooting as he went.

They weren't going to make it—too many bodies and detached limbs in their path, too many bullets, the line of men thinning as they approached the gray wall. Thomas refused to accept it; he wouldn't process the ruin.

Don't think, just move.

He fought the smoke assaulting his chest as his lungs screamed for fresh air. His burning eyes strained to see through the murky haze of smoky blackness.

All Thomas saw were recurrent sparks from guns firing down. Forced to the ground to evade flying Minie balls, Thomas loaded his weapon from a little depression in the frigid, shaking earth, fired as best he could, and shrunk down for protection after each shot.

A desperate, frustrated yelp escaped from Thomas's throat when an officer called retreat. Thomas was determined to get up and move forward, not willing to give up, but a pull on his overcoat settled the matter, Robert forcing him to move backwards.

The gruesome journey down the hill commenced as the sky darkened, nightfall creeping in. Thomas's face contorted grotesquely as he stepped on the bodies of wounded comrades. Their cries haunted him.

"Follow me, Tom," Robert whistled behind him. "I'll make a path."

Thomas tried, but the night blacked out most of his vision. He was trying to match his brother's pace when his knee knocked into a soldier's head. He wasn't lying down but crouched like a baby, crying and shaking.

Thomas knelt down to assist, figuring the soldier was too scared to move. He descended to his knees and stumbled at the sight. It was Henry.

"Are you wounded?" Thomas reached out to touch him. The quake in his body was intense and rapid and his uniform was wet. Thomas felt around and discovered no wounds. Henry sobbed.

"It's over now, Henry," Thomas reassured him. "Come on. I'll help you get back down the hill."

"My mama, can ya fetch her for me, China boy?" His body shook and sweat dripped from his head, despite the cold.

"Sure, Henry. What do you say about us getting back down the hill first?"

Henry nodded and took Thomas's outstretched arm. Thomas positioned himself under Henry's armpit and wrapped one arm around his thick waist. They hobbled back up and over the hills, most composed of soldiers' bodies in heaps and not the natural terrain.

When they returned to the Fourteenth, they were greeted by a crowd. Henry let go of Thomas, his fear instantly abating.

"You get lost Henry?" James ran up. "God almighty, we were getting ready to declare you amongst the dead."

The group seemed to wait for answer, which Henry didn't have.

"I got a bit stuck," Thomas pronounced. "Henry had to help me out of a tight spot."

"Ah, China boy. Didn't see you there with that black hair against the night," James smirked. "Seems to me you lost your will. Guess you are yellow like your skin."

"Maybe you're right, James." Thomas had no fight left in him. He gathered his musket and departed, leaving the group and the horrendous heights behind. Henry watched him go.

Shrouded in an oppressive misery in the following days, the regiment moved in a state of disbelief, the dreadful reality of the battle sinking in. Thomas and the others barely spoke. Sleep was their only relief and then only until the ghastly visions from Marye's Heights invaded their dreams.

The solitary light in the darkness came from the comfort Thomas felt around the evening fire sitting near to Elias. Henry hadn't welcomed him to the group, but he didn't go so far as to exclude him either. Thomas figured it was Henry's way of saying thanks. Either way, it suited Thomas fine in the moment. The fire was enough. He was too exhausted to desire more.

Four days after the battle, as the boys settled in to feel the fire's warmth and hear its comforting crackle and pop, the heavens opened up a drenching rain. Soaked and freezing, their only heat source extinguished, Thomas figured Nature's actions were appropriate for their mournful mood.

CHAPTER THIRTEEN

Thomas re-braided his long, dark locks alongside an icy creek, a mile or so from camp. He'd slipped away as the boys built up their cook fires. The slaughter at Fredericksburg had wearied the company into silence. The boys slept, ate, and woke without joy—without much ado at all. Although he'd never felt comfortable enough to participate in the camp's camaraderie, he found its absence unbearable.

Thomas desired the cold wind on his face, the trickle of water over ice and rocks, time away to think. He closed his eyes and thought of home. He recalled his chores, his bellyaching about things that seemed trivial now, tasks that were actually luxuries.

He remembered the warm underside of a hen when retrieving her egg, the heat from Barney's back when he groomed the old horse. He thought of smoking birch chips from the family's hearth, scorching flames kissing the bottom of his mama's boiling pot, the aroma of squirrel and potato stew filling the room. The corners of his mouth turned up at the warm memories just as a chilling wind blew through the trees, forcing a shiver. Boy, was it ever cold!

Tomorrow was Christmas Day. If he and Robert were home, they'd be hauling in an overgrown tree to adorn with candles, colorful ribbons, and a string of corn popped at the fire. His pa would read the Gospel of John before presenting the boys with one special gift—usually an exotic trinket brought back from the Orient. Thomas remembered his last Christmas gift: a beautiful ivory elephant.

Thomas finished his braid, the task slowed by frosty fingers. His mama regularly admonished him with pleas to wear his hair shorter, saying the long braid was too much trouble for a boy. But Thomas insisted on keeping it.

Once, after Thomas had been with the Beck family for a year, Joseph returned from sea. Thomas had peppered him with questions.

"Pa, tell me about the boys in China. Have they braided pigtails like me?"

"Aye, my boy, yes. They are called *bian zi*. Theirs are just like yours."

From that point on, Joseph confirmed the fact after every voyage.

"Good, Pa," Thomas would say, touching it. "Good."

Thomas remembered little else from his other life, but he kept his queue. He couldn't part with it, not without severing something deep inside him. When others saw him, they always noticed it—how black, how long, and how tightly wound its strands.

The differences between Thomas and the others didn't end there, but they all seemed to settle upon it. He couldn't change his small, thin frame, the slant of his eyes, or the yellow tinge of his skin, so why change his hair?

Despite everything about him that seemed so un-American, Thomas didn't *feel* Chinese. He *felt* like a Connecticut boy, a Yankee. The men would definitely laugh at that. Thomas found himself chuckling, too.

How do you feel like a person? You either are or you aren't. That's the point, isn't it? If Negroes are people, and anybody can see that they are, then they have rights. That's what President Lincoln proclaimed, and that's what we're fighting for—what I'm fighting for.

Now, if they could only figure out how to win.

Winter camp took on the appearance of a small village, dirt paths arranged in a crisscross pattern. Cabin rows of soldiers' homes intersected with erected churches and sutler shops. The sutlers trailed the army, followed wherever it went. As soon as the fighting stopped, they parked their wagons, set up their stands, and sold their wares. Thomas generally avoided them and thought it strange that men would choose profit over fighting for the cause. But, as he observed men buying newspapers, playing cards, and blankets, he saw that it brought his comrades a small measure of comfort. Thomas couldn't begrudge anyone that.

He wished he had brought along a photo of his mama, or one of his pa's oriental bottles or spices. It would be nice to have something to hold on to. Thomas shrugged. It was a very real possibility that he'd have to abandon them on the march or that he would lose them in the heat of battle. He might even be forced to surrender them to eager soldiers looking for something to gamble.

Better that they are home safe, Thomas figured. *I'll focus on getting back to my family—people matter more than things.*

People! Thomas was struck with a startling and sudden need to find the medical tent. Thomas changed direction and reached it quickly. He stepped inside and was greeted by a ghastly stench. Thomas masked his mouth and nose with the back of his hand as he approached the surgeon. He resembled a professor—at least what Thomas pictured one looking like from books he'd read—spectacles low on the bridge of a narrow nose. He sat on a barrel, next to a table turned into a makeshift desk, making notations with a pencil.

"Excuse me, sir?"

"What can I do for you, boy?" The surgeon looked up.

"Um, the black man, sir, my brother and I brought to you before the battle. Is he still here?"

The surgeon motioned down a row of litters, pointed to the last one. Thomas inquired after his condition.

"He will recover, most likely." The surgeon leaned back in his chair and slowly removed his glasses. "Seems the bullet merely grazed him. I cleaned the wound, patched it up. Same with his wounds on his back. He's been talking in his sleep, groaning. Now, if you'll excuse me, I've got to see to the rest of our soldiers. Dysentery never sleeps."

Thomas nodded. As the surgeon turned to check on his patients, Thomas approached the litter and found the man awake, watching him.

"Hello." Thomas's voice quivered. "How are you doing, sir?"

"I'm a long ways tired, but Sam's gonna make it, thankest to you." The man spoke fast, in a manner that Thomas had trouble understanding.

"I'm pleased to hear that. Is Sam your name?"

"That'd be," he said, "What's your'n?

"Thomas." He knelt down by the man's side. "Sam, forgive me for asking, but are you a runaway?" Sam's eyes darted around. "Don't worry—you are safe here."

"My wife died with our'n little child." Sam's voice was weak. "Somethin' awful. It wrecked me; I couldn't work the plow no more. Mass'r got to whippin' me and I ran when the sun went down. Ain't goin' back."

"What will you do?"

"I'm a gonna help your'n army make us free." Sam tried to sit up, pointed to Thomas's face. "You lookee different than them other soldiers."

"I came from another country called China." Thomas pulled his braid to rest on his chest so Sam could see. "But I'm an American now."

"Them blue soldiers acceptin' of you?"

"Not at first," Thomas admitted. "Maybe not now. But I'm a soldier either way."

"What're you fighting for?"

"Freedom." Thomas gave the simplest answer. "For you," he said, "and for me."

"Praise be, Lord Almighty." Sam reached his hand to Thomas, and Thomas took it. Warmth radiated from his palm and Thomas squeezed, placed his other hand on top of theirs.

The regiment's Christmas celebrations were muted, but Thomas appreciated the attempt to acknowledge the day. The quartermaster requisitioned some fresh potatoes and some fine, fat Virginia hams to fill the soldiers' hungry bellies. The men, strengthened by the good food and comforted by the familiar hymns the band played, began to shake off the weariness from Fredericksburg.

Flanked by his brother and Elias, Thomas took a hearty bite of his meat, then went in for another. The sweet and moving harmony of *O Holy Night* filled the air around them, and the voices paused to listen, many seeming to hear the second verse for the first time.

Truly he taught us to love one another,

His law is love and His gospel is peace.

Chains shall He break, for the slave is our brother.

And in His name, all oppression shall cease.

Thomas gulped. He could see by the look in other men's eyes that those words meant more while fighting in the war. Thomas glanced down at what remained of his Christmas dinner. He found his knapsack and wrapped what was left inside. He would take it to Sam tomorrow to wish him a Merry Christmas. The birth of their Savior was, as Scripture said, a light for the world, even in the midst of darkness.

Soon it would be 1863. It would be a new year, a fresh start, a beginning. Mr. Lincoln's Emancipation Proclamation would officially take effect. Thomas's eyes glazed over, becoming reflective, as he considered that. To Sam and his people, he figured the president must appear Christ-like, coming to break their bonds. And Yankee soldiers, Thomas considered, were to be his instruments of peace.

CHAPTER FOURTEEN

"You figuring on wearing that Chinaman?"

The sutler was a substantial man with a thick chest and stark black beard. He pointed at the shirt that Thomas held up to inspect. Thomas had disappeared behind it.

Thomas checked the shirt's seams, felt for worn patches in the fabric. Satisfied it would do the job, he picked up the largest cap he could find.

"I'll take it," Thomas said to the sutler. "And this cap, too."

"You sure?" the sutler asked. "These things are too big for you. I ain't got children's clothes."

"They aren't for me," Thomas stated matter-of-factly. He

dropped some coins into the man's massive palm, twice as much as it cost before the war, but dismissed it with a shrug. Thomas tucked the items inside his uniform coat and nodded to the man, who still wore a bewildered look.

"Hiya, Thomas." Elias came walking up the lane. His arms were crossed over his long chest, and his cheeks were red from the cool wind. "Where are you headed off to?"

"Morning, Elias. I'm headed to see Sam at the medical tent."

"May I join you? I'd like to meet him."

"Of course. He'll enjoy the company. He's likely growing tired of me."

Thomas and Elias passed by a surgeon's table filled with medical instruments that looked more like a carpenter's tools—saws, clamps, and drills. Thomas watched as Elias registered their uses.

"Wretched place," Elias noted.

"Must be terrible during battle," Thomas agreed. "I heard they saw off limbs and toss them in a nearby field. I think I'd rather meet my judgment than endure that."

"I'd choose neither, if I had a choice."

The pair stepped through the tent flaps. Thomas pointed down the line of stretchers and led Elias that way.

"Afternoon, Sam." Thomas tipped his hat with two fingers.

"Thomas." Sam sat up in the cot. "It does me good to see you."

"Sam, I'd like to introduce you to my bunkmate, Elias. He came to say hello."

"Pleased to meet you." Elias removed his cap.

Sam nodded a greeting.

"I brought you something." Thomas handed Sam the shirt and cap.

"Why's that, Thomas? You's don't needs it no more?"

"Doc says you're fixing to leave on account of you're feeling better. I can't let you brave this cold with a tattered shirt."

Sam was visibly moved and had trouble finding words. Thomas reached out and patted his shoulder.

"Now, you let me know when you're up to it. We'll find us a checkerboard somewhere and you'll make good on your bet."

"Sure's will, Thomas." Sam bobbed his head.

"And I'll play the winner," Elias added.

A horde of boys scampered by as Thomas and Elias emerged from the tent, nearly knocking them off their feet.

"Hey, where ya'll off to?"

"Henry's been running his mouth all day about something he wants to show us." Robert grabbed Thomas in stride. Thomas sped up to meet their pace and glanced at Elias, who scuttled alongside.

"Keep up, boys."

Fred and William came jogging from behind and took their place with Henry and James at the head of the group. The boys made their way to the outskirts of camp, near the pickets.

"What's going on?" Thomas whispered to his brother.

"Quiet, Tommy-boy," Henry admonished him.

They reached a bank near water. Henry cupped his hands over his mouth, tilted his neck upward. He let out three owl-like hoots in rapid succession.

A quick moment later, Thomas heard a similar-sounding hoot returned, but softer, obviously from across the pond.

"Who's that?"

The calls came again. Thomas saw a flash of gray.

"Henry! Are those Rebs?" Thomas elbowed Robert. "What in the heavens is he doing?"

"It's harmless, Tommy-boy," Henry assured him. "They're bored like us. They called over awhile back looking to barter for some coffee. You'll see."

Just then Thomas noticed the small burlap sack tied to Henry's waist. Henry pointed to the water. A little canoe, shaped out of a block of wood, was teetering its way over to the bank. It had a small sail made out of an old handkerchief and a sack in its bed.

It was a long journey for the little boat, but none of the boys said a word as it made its way, except for small gasps when a slight breeze threatened to capsize her. When it came close enough, Henry retrieved it from the water.

He removed the sack inside and unraveled a note wrapped around it.

"Enjoy the blow, Billy Yank." Henry passed the note around. He removed the coffee bag from his waist line and put it in the boat.

"Someone give me a pencil." Fred, Robert's bunkmate, handed him one. Henry tore some cloth from his undershirt and scribed his own return note.

"Thank ya kindly for the tobacco, Johnny Reb. See ya at the war."

Thomas blew into his fisted hands and flexed his stiff fingers. He picked the jar of ink from a sanded log and gave it a shake. It wasn't easy to pen letters on these January evenings, but the freezing ink wasn't the real issue.

He couldn't figure out what to write...the whiteness of the parchment stared at him, even as dusk settled. Flickers of firelight danced across the page, reflecting his jumbled thoughts. Bartering with the Rebs...how strange.

Thomas didn't like to think about the enemy. To him, they were one thing and one thing only: obstacles standing in the way of freedom for all.

But deep down, he knew the men across the way were just that...men. They were husbands and fathers and brothers and sons, just like him. They fought for their way of life. He did his best to forget that when they marched toward him in battle.

"Whatcha writing there, Thomas?" Elias grabbed a seat next to him.

"Oh, nothing yet." Thomas set down the parchment and pointed out ahead. "Looks like Henry is back. He's got a grin as wide as the Potomac River. Guess he enjoyed the Rebel tobacco."

"Hey, Tommy-boy, Elias. Thanks for keeping the fire hot for us." Henry winked while patting James on the back. "Now, that was an enjoyable way to pass the evenin'."

"Glad you had a fine time," Elias returned. "You worry at all about conversing with those Rebs, Henry?"

"Nah. We've got ourselves a truce—we won't shoot until the generals start the war again. James and me are gonna get closer next time so that we can actually talk with them boys."

"Henry, why are you doing this?" Thomas felt his body tense. "What's the point of talking with them today when you're probably gonna have to shoot at them tomorrow?"

"Why do you spend your days with that Negro?" Henry accused him. "Is there a point to that? He's still a slave."

"No, he's not—not anymore. He's a person, Henry."

"So ya say. I reckon the Rebs are people, too."

"They are the enemy!"

"Maybe, but that runaway—he's the reason for the blasted war." Henry pointed at Elias. "Boys on both sides are dying over his precious freedom. Ya think he's got a future, slave or free? Freed men up North ain't much better off than them slaves. Maybe they even got it worse. I hear the slaves get three meals a day, no matter what, and a bed to sleep in. It's..."

Henry paused, a flash of sadness flickering in his blue eyes.

"It's better than what some of us have had."

"That's not the point, Henry," Elias interjected. "He has a chance now to make his own way."

"Like that matters?" Henry spat. "It don't mean nothing if he starves trying to find work. Anyways, that Negro ain't gonna be here long. I'm sure his master's got a posse out looking for him, offering a big reward. Just a matter of time and he's gonna have to go back."

"I would never let that happen," Thomas announced, standing up.

A large chortle filled the circle of men.

"Oh, Tommy-boy." Henry held his stomach to control his laughing fit. "You break me up."

CHAPTER FIFTEEN

"She said yes. God bless me, she said yes!"

Thomas's lips formed a smile, a native reaction to happiness filling his ears. Elias rushed toward them, a letter high in his fist. Henry looked up from his whittling of a flute. James put down his book.

"Who said yes, Elias?" Thomas asked. "What's got you so excited?"

"My Sarah, she has agreed to marry me." Elias skidded to a stop. "Can you believe it? My sweetheart, Miss Sarah Diana Harrington, has consented to become my wife."

Thomas grabbed Elias by the arm and the two embraced. The brightness in Elias's blue eyes and the joy in his voice all touched

Thomas deeply. He felt a penetrating swath of emotion, genuine delight at Elias's news. He knew they had become friends.

"Didn't know that you proposed marriage." James stood up and extended a hand.

"After Fredericksburg." Elias removed his cap. "Too close of a call. Made me wonder what I was waiting for. We've been sweethearts since we were young'uns. This is mighty fine...time to get this war won so I can get on home to her."

"Where will you live?" Henry carved shavings from his instrument.

"I'll work to buy some of my pa's land and build us a house. We'll raise our family near my kin. I'd like a boy first. My Sarah will be a most tender mother."

"While you get yourself hitched," James picked his teeth, "I'll be moving out to the western territories to hang my shingle as a blacksmith. Always wanted to do that."

Henry said he'd keep trying to make his way as a carpenter.

"So what's a China boy to do?" Henry motioned at Thomas. "Hey, you ever kiss a girl there, Tommy?"

"I don't see how that concerns you," Thomas managed, despite the heat rushing to his face.

"That means he ain't," Henry cackled. "Maybe you gotta wait to get back to your own country and find a Chinese girl and have lots of yellow, pigtailed babies."

"This *is* my country." Thomas gritted his teeth. "Why else would I fight?"

"Look around, Tommy. There ain't nobody around like ya. Even the slaves have their own kind. Injuns got their own tribes, too. Ya think you're gonna find a white woman to marry ya? Or, maybe you'd prefer a Negro woman? Geez, Tommy, ya even think about it?"

"I think," Thomas's chin was set, "that you ought to mind your own affairs."

"Ya ain't got no prospects of finding a girl in America, China boy. You outta face it now and figure out a way to get back home."

Thomas started to protest that he was home, but instead he kicked an errant log into the fire, kicking up sparks in the air. He departed for the woods.

"Ah, come back, Tommy," Henry called. "I bet your pa will go over and get ya a wife, bring her back from sea just like he did ya."

Thomas was bound for his special place alongside the creek north of camp. It was bit of a walk, but it allowed him time alone. Sometimes it was just too loud in camp—or was the noise inside his head?

He'd grown tired of defending who he was and why he was fighting, almost as much as he was sick of the winter. It was early March, but the cold had been content to stay.

The repeating sound of a hammer's thwack turned Thomas's attention toward a meadow full of felled trees where men were slinging axes and sawing logs. The wind blew a spray of sawdust near his face. Thomas rubbed his eyes.

A closer look and Thomas realized the men were Negroes, their sleeves rolled up, sweat dripping from their brows. More and more runaway slaves had joined their ranks, and the men had been put to work on camp duties alongside the soldiers. These men were obviously repairing wagons and ammunition trunks, crates for foodstuffs, furniture for the officers. Sam was among the other men, carrying an ax he set aside when he saw Thomas. Sam strode his way.

"Hiya, Thomas." Sam wiped his hands on a handkerchief as he

approached. He extended a hand.

"Why, Sam, I didn't know you were a carpenter." Thomas shook Sam's hand.

"Learned me lots on the plantation." Sam tucked the handkerchief in his back pocket. "Masser says 'do it' and you's figure out some ways."

"I suppose that's true." Thomas studied the set. "Do you know any of these men? I mean, did you know them before?"

"Can't says that I did. Met some kindly folks, though. Guess you can say we gots some things in common."

"Yes, that must be nice." Thomas recalled Henry's comment about his being the only Chinese in America. "Are they happy here?"

"Better'n being a slave." Sam turned his attention back to Thomas. "This'n just for now. We wants to join the fight."

"Become soldiers?"

"Yessir. Some Negro troops are forming in some place...Massa...Massa—"

"Massachusetts?"

"Yes, thankee. We thinks it won't be too long before your

commanding general lets us fight here."

"I hope you get your chance, Sam."

The rhythm of men working the ends of a two-man saw accompanied the workers' rendition of the great battle hymn of the republic, *John Brown's Body*:

"Glory, Glory, Hallelujah

Glory, Glory, Hallelujah

Glory, Glory, Hallelujah

His soul is marching on.

John Brown was John the Baptist of the Christ we are to see,

Christ who of the bondmen shall the Liberator be,

And soon throughout the Sunny South the slaves shall all be free,

For his soul is marching on.

Glory, Glory, Hallelujah

Glory, Glory, Hallelujah

Glory, Glory, Hallelujah

His soul is marching on.

The conflict that he heralded he looks from heaven to view,

On the army of the Union with its flag red, white, and blue.

And heaven shall ring with anthems o'er the deed they mean to do,

For his soul is marching on."

Thomas and Sam were enraptured by the majestic tune. Thomas recalled the headlines about John Brown. The ardent abolitionist had been found guilty of inciting insurrection before the war and been hanged. Standing there with Sam, who was humming along, Thomas realized what Brown's efforts to free the slaves had meant to them.

"Masser Lincoln's freed us in the North and we wants to fight so we's can go back home again."

"Back South, you mean. And what then, Sam?"

"Don't matter."

"Why not?"

"Freedom's got to be first. The rest be figureds out later."

Thomas casted a line out into the frigid water. He'd found a discarded mucket in camp and fashioned the wire bail into a fish hook. He'd tried to soften some hard tack by soaking it in water to use as bait, but it had disintegrated. Still, fishing with just a hook was worth a try. Maybe, just maybe, he could have a fish dinner instead of a dry biscuit flavored with leftover bacon grease.

"Evening, brother."

"Evening." Thomas rose from his squat to greet Robert. Time with his brother was the real reason he loved this spot at the creek.

"Catchin' anything?"

"Just a chill." Thomas shuddered. "Spring is just around the corner, right?"

"Yep—just in time to turn this hard ground into a swampy,

muddy mess for the march."

"Happy thought." Thomas punched his brother in the arm.

"Well, at least we'll be doing something. This has been the longest winter ever."

"Hey, Robert, you ever kiss a girl?"

"Why in tarnation ya asking that?" Thomas noted a hint of sheepishness from his usually confident older sibling.

"Curious is all. Elias just got engaged."

"Oh, well, bully for him. Bet he's ready to get back home."

"After the war's won, yes. He wants to see the end of slavery first. But at least he knows what comes after it."

"And ya don't? Figured you go home to Ma and work the farm, like always."

"Is that what you'll do? Will you be a farmer?"

"Maybe, or a merchant sailor like Pa."

"Get married?"

"Well, maybe."

"Wish I had that option." Thomas pulled his twine from the water.

"Why wouldn't ya?"

"Henry says no young lady will want to spend time with a Chinese boy, er, man."

Thomas hoped Henry was wrong about that, but he had his doubts. Henry was right about no other Chinese people being in the entire country, North or South. Thomas had never seen anyone like him. Even Elias had said Thomas was a peculiar thing. He must appear that way to everyone.

"Once a Chinese Yankee, always a Chinese Yankee, I suppose."

"Guess I never thought of it that way," Robert acknowledged. "Bet it feels kinda lonely."

"Never did before," Thomas admitted, "but then again, I never knew anyone but you, Mama, and Pa." He recalled the beautiful girl from the grand review of troops and let go a long sigh.

"Do you wish you were someone else?"

"Well, I...." Thomas thought a minute. He really didn't. His mama's words came back to him about God fashioning him the way he intended. Pa had said Thomas was the son he chose. He knew there was something extraordinary and special about that.

"I suppose not."

"Somebody's got to be first," Robert stated matter-of-factly.

"Beg pardon?"

"First," Robert repeated. "This country's full of all kinds of different people, but we're all Americans, right? At some point, when the first Europeans came over here, someone had to be the first of their kind. Might be kind of an honor when ya think of it that way."

"You really think so?"

"Yep, I do. And I think you're the right one to do it."

Thomas wanted to ask how that was, with all the ribbing and insults he was constantly deflecting, but Robert kept on.

"I couldn't do it as well as ya. I woulda been court-martialed for fighting by now. Must be what God meant for ya to do. That's what Mama would say, anyhow."

Words failed Thomas. He stretched his arm over to his brother and shook his hand.

"Thank you, brother." Robert returned the gesture.

"I didn't do nothin'."

"Yes, you did. May I ask another question?

"Nothin's stopped ya so far."

"What can you tell me about that kiss?"

CHAPTER SIXTEEN

The president was coming! The message passed through the ranks of the army like a wildfire during a drought. Adorned in dress suits, the Fourteenth trekked on eager feet, leaving their winter camp behind.

Thomas's senses delighted on the march. The troops buzzed with excitement, delirious for their moment in front of the president. Thomas longed to lay eyes on Mr. Lincoln—to perhaps even be seen by him, by the courageous man who led their country.

His mind fluttering with possibilities, Thomas allowed himself a passing fancy to daydream about having an audience with the general-in-chief. A man like Lincoln had deep compassion for his fellow man and an unwavering commitment to freedom. His

Emancipation Proclamation proved that. Not only had Mr. Lincoln declared freedom for the slaves, he had acknowledged their worth as persons by allowing them to join the fight for their cause.

Abraham Lincoln. Thomas had an inkling that this man would welcome meeting a Chinese Yankee. This man would applaud his service to America. This man would understand why Thomas chose to fight. He might even be inclined to offer his hand and proffer words unthinkable to other men, words such as these: *thank you.*

Thomas bumped his forehead with the palm of his hand, as if to smack some sense into his head. He wasn't going to speak with the president. He probably wouldn't even get a glimpse of him; taller soldiers in front would block his view. Still, Thomas delighted in the notion and allowed it to comfort and warm him as he marched. He stepped proudly as the sunlight gleamed off his polished bayonet.

When they had marched just shy of four miles, the men of the Fourteenth Connecticut filed into a wide plain pressed into service as the parade ground. Four at a time, the men joined the ranks of the Army of the Potomac, men from Pennsylvania and New York, Maine and New Jersey.

"Heads forward, eyes to the front"—hushed orders were issued through sergeants' pursed lips. Impossible. The war would be over before another chance like this.

Thomas pressed his shoulders back, tightened his neck muscles to fix his head straight. But his eyes darted around. The cheery music from the band came from his left, so Thomas's eyes strained that way. He looked among the bystanders, the men standing still on the side, not moving with the troops' blue wave. Among the proper suits and wagons, he searched for the president's tall, black hat, the one reprinted in the newspapers. Finding nothing, he fought against disappointment and kept up the march.

A waving American flag whipped through Thomas's field of vision. He located it and followed it down to a view of officers' hats and gold tassels. A cluster of men on horseback came toward him, moving in a slow trot. Thomas noted an officer's stark white, gloved hand. It held a cigar with two fingers and palmed a horse's reins with the rest. Then he saw it—the black hat.

Thomas spied President Lincoln on a beautiful chestnut horse, plainly adorned with a dusty and faded blanket underneath a worn saddle. The president's long limbs were cramped into tight stirrups so that his knobby knees rode high on the animal. Whomever had loaned the president his horse had been considerably shorter than its current rider.

Thomas watched the president with wonder. He blinked to test the image, to make sure it was really there. The trappings of the horse seemed unfit for a man of his stature, but so did the president himself.

The hem of Mr. Lincoln's pant leg was splotched with mud; the black cotton was wrinkled and caught up a bit, revealing some of the president's pale leg. Without his signature tall hat, Abraham Lincoln might have been just another onlooker—some reporter or county lawyer out to take in the grand review. But, no, he carried himself with a humble, quiet authority that stunned Thomas into a stupor. He could only stare.

The president nodded to the troops as he passed by them, one lanky arm outstretched in a little wave. He spoke words that Thomas could not hear, a fact that would have deeply disappointed Thomas had he been able to think on it. Instead, he marched onward, drawing nearer to the president with every rhythmic step, his heart beating out of his chest.

As the Fourteenth Connecticut marched past President Lincoln, Thomas felt a fluttering, fast jolt in his heart, as if walking the road to Calvary with the son of God himself. He straightened his shoulders back again and held his breath and his head high. Thomas didn't remember taking another breath until they returned to camp later that night.

The regimental band played into the wee hours of the morning. The men were like children on Christmas morning, dancing and singing without a care. Thomas had never heard some of the gleeful, cheery songs the band played this night. *Oh, Susanna* and *Buffalo Gals* were certainly different from the mournful and lonely camp songs he knew or the *Battle Cry of Freedom* played often on the march, but Thomas found he liked them—a lot. He couldn't help but slap his knee to match the beat.

Banging their tin cups and canteens, the boys laughed and drank while their comrades danced around the fire. Henry and James were up, arms around shoulders, swaying, moving, and dancing to the music. Thomas was enjoying the easy revelry when he noted Henry's wide, beaming smirk directed straight at him.

Thomas's own smile made haste and he looked down, fully expecting a lashing of words about joining in with the celebration. Instead, Henry pulled him from his seat on the ground.

"It's your turn, Tommy-boy," Henry announced to the group. "Let's have a China boy show us a monkey dance."

To Thomas's surprise, the normal dejection he felt when called a monkey dissipated. Henry had his arm around Thomas now, a strong-smelling libation in his cup, and a smile that bristled with joy—the same as everyone else. There was nothing mean in the words this night. And, Thomas could now admit, his queue *was* tail-like, long and black, and unusual for a soldier.

The band played *Camptown Races.*

"The Camptown ladies sing this song,
Doo-da, Doo-da
The Camptown racetrack's five miles long
Oh, de doo-da day

Goin' to run all night
Goin' to run all day
I bet my money on a bob-tailed nag
Somebody bet on the gray."

"Alright, I can do this." Thomas whispered beneath his breath.

Thomas took a cautious step into the circle. With a giant leap of faith, he crouched and made a springy leap into the air. He hopped up and down with his arms curled under his armpits. By performing monkey jumps and bellowing primate squawks and squeals, Thomas imitated Henry's antics from that long ago day in Washington City. His belly flopped as he did his monkey impression, as much from nerves as from his own uncontrollable laugher. He had his comrades in stitches. Their laughter bounced through the trees in the night.

His bunkmates had finally fallen into sleep, but Thomas couldn't rest. Thoughts swirled through his mind. He retrieved his writing pad, slipped out past his bunkmates, and went back out to the fire. He fanned the embers, blew on them, and added more tinder. The built-up fire and the soft glow from a full moon shed enough light on his paper for him to pen a letter.

Thomas bent down to lie on his stomach and used a flat rock to support his paper. He chuckled as he dipped his pen, recalling his dance and the weight it took off, the president's long legs stuck in the short stirrups of the horse.

Dear Mama,

I write as the night has turned to day. It must be near two o'clock in the morning, and yet I cannot sleep. Today we had an audience with President Abraham Lincoln himself—can you believe it? He traveled from Washington to review the army. I expected to see him with some great accompaniment, but he rode a simple horse, waving to us. What an inspiration he was! The shindy afterward just ended, with men nearly falling into their bedrolls. I enjoyed myself immensely and even danced a little— don't tell Pa, for I fear it might be as embarrassing to hear as I feel to write of it.

I was glad to hear of Pa's safe return in your last letter. Yes, Robert and I are staying warm. The huts were a god-send, and the fires were always ablaze. It was good to go back on the march. It's been a long spell since Fredericksburg. Four months is too long to think on that. I am eager for the next battle. Now that the Emancipation Proclamation is in effect, we need to win this war.

Robert and I discovered a runaway while on picket duty. He had gashes on his back from a master's whip. Ms. Stowe's book told tale of slavery's evil, but now I have seen it for myself.

I've gotten to know Sam now—that's his name. He noticed the difference in me from other soldiers. For once, I was glad of it. I told him that I'm fighting for freedom. Freedom for him and freedom for me. I wonder what that really means. What will happen when the war ends?

I never gave it much thought before, figuring I'd just stay with you on the farm. I'm afraid now that is not enough. Please understand, Mama, for you know my affection.

You taught me about the Declaration—about equality endowed by God and unalienable rights—life, liberty, and the pursuit of happiness. It's plain as day that we're fighting for our lives and for liberty. But the third part tortures me. May I be permitted to pursue my happiness here? Will Sam? What will the slaves' freedom be like?

Henry says they would be better off staying in bonds, that food and shelter would be easier if masters provided it. I disagree. Sam had the gashes and scars to prove there is nothing more important than freedom, whatever way it can come.

The soldiers of old—pa and great grand pap Thomas, who fought in the Revolution, they knew freedom wasn't perfect or easy. They saw men die for it, as we are fighting and dying now. If I've found freedom here, it has been a hard one, and yet I'm reluctant to give it up. I won't give it up.

Pa saved me from something like slavery once. We'll end slavery for good if we can win this war. We'll expand freedom. That's why I'm fighting, Mama. Robert helped me to see that maybe, just maybe, my being a Chinese Yankee will convince the boys that being an American is not about where you came from or what you look like, but about the freedom we help to spread.

Thomas put down his pen. He thought for a moment and then tore the letter into pieces, slowly, carefully, reverently. Thomas knew deep in his heart that he'd written the truth. That's why he couldn't send it home—not yet—not until the war was won.

CHAPTER SEVENTEEN

Thomas slugged off his cap and wiped the sweat from his brow. He fell gently into a sweet little spot on a hill, a good place to scrape the mud from his boots. Thomas was bone tired after a day of drill, yet a smile spread across his face. It was a good feeling, this kind of tired. It wasn't the long, drudging exhaustion of winter and waiting, but the work of increased drills and tactics and target practice. The kind of work that meant something was about to happen.

The heat had come on quickly, seeming to make up for its prolonged absence. Perhaps it was the afterglow of seeing the president, or the simple joy of springtime—the blossoming of the Virginia ground from gray to green, from barren to blooming—that created the hopeful atmosphere. But deep down, Thomas knew it was more than that. It came from knowing more about his purpose in the army. He understood better from Sam, from Robert, even from Henry, that he was doing something important.

Robert had said Thomas was the first Chinese soldier, maybe the first Chinese person in America. He felt an emerging pride about that. His father often said that nothing worth doing was easy. His mama's litany of scripture verses about the persecuted being blessed scrolled through his thoughts. Even President Lincoln was hated by many because he represented an end to slavery in the South, but Thomas had no doubt about his eventual legacy and impact on the nation—if they could win the war.

Nothing mattered more to Thomas. Drill and springtime and even the muck coating his pants meant action was coming. And this time, the men of the Army of the Potomac were being led by a man known for his willingness to fight. After the slaughter at Fredericksburg, President Lincoln had replaced General Burnside in favor of General Joseph Hooker. The troops knew about Fighting Joe's reputation for taking care of his soldiers, making sure they had enough food and munitions. They also knew he would take the battle directly to Confederate General Robert Edward Lee.

Thomas stared at the checkerboard. Sam had just executed a move of two double jumps that succeeded in completely wiping the board clean of his red checkers. He looked up at Sam, who leaned back against the tree stump, folded his arms, and smiled.

"Sam's gotcha scratching yours head, Thomas."

"That you do, Sam." Thomas laughed out loud. "You wiped me out like a general firing cannons in an exposed field. But the war's not over yet. Another game?"

A bugle blared in the distance and their heads turned.

"Tom!" Robert ran toward them. "Fighting Joe's orders came down. We're moving out."

"I'm coming." Thomas rose to his feet. He had to make fast tracks back to camp. It would already be breaking, and he would need to clean his musket and tighten his bundle. Thomas turned to Sam, who got up to meet his outstretched arm.

"See you after the battle." Thomas shook Sam's hand.

"Farewell, Thomas. You's a good friend. If'n we don't meets again, Sam's wanting you's to know that."

"I'm coming back, Sam. I'll see you after the battle."

"Good Lord's not promised tomorrow for us."

"I know, but I expect to see you soon." Thomas spied the checkerboard. "Do me a favor, will you, my friend?"

Thomas gathered the checkers into a small burlap sack and handed the board to Sam.

"It's too cumbersome for the march, but take care of it. You owe me a re-match."

"God goes with you, Thomas." Sam retrieved the board from Thomas and gave him a half-hearted smile. "Sam's gonna keep it safe and you's right, we'll meet again."

Thomas reached up to pat Sam on the shoulder before setting off in a sprint back to camp. As he did, Sam whispered, "even if it be at heaven's gates."

Outfitted with eight days' rations, the boys marched ten miles in two days through the flowering Virginia landscape. When they reached the muddy brown waters of the Rapidan River, they crossed it via a ford and embarked on an overland route that took them to within one mile of the Chancellor House, the center of a village so named Chancellorsville. Word had passed down the line that General Hooker had established his headquarters there. It filled the boys with excitement and anticipation.

The Fourteenth Connecticut had settled in to make camp when word reached them about a surprise twilight attack on the Eleventh Corps by feared Confederate General Stonewall Jackson, the hero of the first battle of Bull Run Creek.

The Fourteenth marched double-quick to help, running as the awful shrieks of the Rebel yell filled their guts with dread. When they arrived, breathless, they were horrified at what they saw.

They were too late. The soldiers of the Eleventh Corps had been caught completely off-guard. With their muskets stacked up against their bed rolls, the boys had been cooking their dinners over open fires as the sun sank down. When the gray mass had torn through with that blood-curdling scream, most of the men were without their guns, some even without their boots.

The once-peaceful camp had become a grotesque graveyard, soldiers' bodies on the ground where they were shot. Some of the cook fires still had flame, and yet, they were no longer being tended. Thomas couldn't help but stare at a dead soldier whose tin coffee cup lay just out of his reach.

As horrible as it was to see the dead, Thomas clamped his eyelids against the horror-filled looks in the eyes of the survivors. He had seen those looks before—at Antietam, his first battle, and that awful day in Fredericksburg. But nothing looked quite like this...soldiers in shock, beaten before they had a chance to fight.

There was little time to process that before orders came to meet new fire coming from the right. The Fourteenth redeployed, but were stopped again mid-march and repositioned by officers. When orders finally came through to shelter for the night, many of the men simply dropped down where they stood.

"It doesn't seem right to attack a man while he's making his supper." Elias stretched his arms to the stars. "It's not humane."

"Any means to win," Thomas mumbled, lost in his thoughts.

"What's that, Thomas?" Robert poked him in the ribs.

"Mama." Thomas looked up. "Remember our last battle on the farm? You used my pigtail to win. Mama said the enemy will use any means."

"I reckon she did. What of it?"

"She was right, is all," Thomas replied, "more than she knew. She probably didn't figure on all the blood."

"Would you want her to, Thomas?" Elias sank into the grass.

"No." Thomas shook his head. "I don't want her to know any of this. She'd be ashamed if she knew how much I want to make them pay. 'Thou shall not kill.' She taught Robert and me the Ten Commandments as surely as pa taught us how to shoot."

"The Bible also says we need to protect the weak," Elias reminded him.

"You ever wonder, Elias," Thomas asked, "how strange it is that both sides of this war pray to the same God, asking for the same protections, the same mercy?"

"Ya'll talk too much, if ya ask me." Robert grabbed a spot next to Elias and Thomas followed. "We signed up as soldiers to fight for our country. We have a duty and so do the Rebel soldiers. God will sort out the judgment when the time comes."

Thomas and Elias exchanged a glance and nodded. Thomas's last thought before sleep overtook him was that he disagreed with his brother on one point. God would surely judge the soldiers, but Thomas had to figure God, while loving the good people of the South, had to side with the North. The South's desire for economic and geographic freedom from Washington City could never trump the North's for human freedom. No just God would side with the slave-owners. Thomas couldn't accept any other truth.

The boys slept until the sun rose over northern Virginia the next morning.

They didn't have to wait long for the fight. Shots from Rebel guns interrupted their slumber. Thomas was enraged, the reminder of yesterday's brutal attack on the Eleventh Corps set his jaw as he grabbed his musket.

The Confederates were firing on the Fourteenth's position, the center of a horseshoe-shaped Union line. The boys fired back through a thick wood, wondering if they were hitting anything at all.

Like target practice with no targets, Thomas thought, but the bullets sailing toward him were real so he shot back with his usual ferocity. The battle grew heated, the armies exchanging blind, but fierce volleys.

"Can't see a darn thing!" a lieutenant yelled. "Well, shoot at the phantom shapes boys....we'll send them back where they came from!"

Thomas's frustration reached a boiling point.

Why can't we see them? Why don't they advance? Do they

have support in the rear? On the flanks?

When the call came to retreat, Thomas stomped into the ground. His cartridge pouch was nearly empty and he wasn't sure they had accomplished anything at all. He still couldn't see.

Thomas drew in a deep, settling breath.

Maybe we aren't retreating, but seeking a better opportunity. Redeploying, yes, maybe that's the plan.

They marched away from the center of the line. Thomas searched for blue troops as his field of vision peeked open a sliver. But he saw no troops on his right and none up ahead. Then he heard the unmistakable rush of water—the Rapidan.

Thomas spat. Victorious soldiers didn't go back in the direction they came. He punched his leg with a clenched fist.

The Yankees crossed back over the river. Down the line came word of the battle's outcome, another terrible defeat. A courier astride a horse galloped fast from the field of battle. Thomas overheard him report to a lieutenant. When he heard "complete rout" from the runner's lips, Thomas feared the worst. The courier completed his hasty report by telling the officer that they had reports of thousands of Union dead.

CHAPTER EIGHTEEN

Thomas lay on his belly inside the tent, his face buried in a wool blanket. The unbearable heat and itchy fabric made him miserable, but he didn't move. He liked the misery—wanted to drown in it. No way would he join his comrades for supper. A mournful rendition of a camp song in the next tent fit his mood better. He submerged his face deeper.

The history books would call the battle of Chancellorsville General Robert E. Lee's best, most complete victory. Back in camp in Falmouth, Virginia, Thomas couldn't summon his enthusiasm for the war, his hope of spreading freedom distant as their wretched losses mounted.

The bugle sounded, shrill and uninviting. Thomas groaned and rolled over. Henry stood holding the tent flap and let the sunshine penetrate through.

"Henry, either come in or get out," Thomas complained, squinting his eyes against the blinding light.

"Still down in the dumps Tommy-boy?" Henry stepped inside.

Grunting, Thomas sat up and rubbed his face.

"So what happened to the boy trying to win the war all by himself? Ya tried to pick off them Rebs in Chancellorsville like a one-man army. Ya losing your will?" Henry bent over to pull on his boots.

"Leave him alone, Henry." Elias closed his Bible.

"Elias, stay out of it. Just wondering here if Tommy's gonna give up." He locked eyes with Thomas.

"I do not give up!" Thomas tightened his fists and confronted Henry, his height hindering him.

"Looks that way to me. Some soldier you turned out to be."

Thomas scrunched his face and forced his hot breath through.

What does Henry know? He fits in here like everyone else. No one questions why he's here or his love for the country. No one taunts him. No one messes with his brother because of him.

"You," Thomas pointed his finger to Henry's chin, "know

nothing about me."

Thomas stormed out of the tent, his fists clenched and his vision blurry with rage. Where could he go? What could he do? Thomas knew who he was and why he was here. He understood what they were fighting for. But they had lost again. How many boys had to die, how many battles would they fight before they'd win another?

Henry followed Thomas down the dirt path.

"Hey, Tommy-boy, ya think ya know everything, don't ya?"

"Henry, I swear, leave me alone."

"Why? Ya keep insisting that ya belong here. Ya say it's your country, your fight, am I right?

"Yes. A hundred times, yes. Even though people like you don't believe it."

"People like me?" Henry scowled at him. "How's that? Just what kind of person ya think I am?

"A mean one. A nasty one. The kind that judges people for stupid reasons—things they can't control."

"Ya ain't the only one that has to deal with stuff they can't control. Ya outta come down off your high horse."

"Beg your pardon?" Thomas was flabbergasted. How could Henry possibly say that about him? He'd never felt superior to anyone in his entire life. He had never looked down on anyone, either.

"I've had it up to here," Henry pushed his hand over his head, "with ya and your kind."

Thomas began to fume, but Henry wasn't finished.

"Your pa saved ya; the entire country fights now to help the Negroes. Ain't no one ever lifted a finger to help me and my little brother when my ma died and my pa just left. We had nothin'. Nothin', ya understand? When your precious slaves were getting fed and sheltered in the South, we were starving."

Thomas stared at the ground. He became distinctly aware that a crowd had started to gather around the patch of dirt where he and Henry confronted each other.

"I didn't know that, Henry."

"Never bothered to ask, ya mean."

"How could I? You've had it out for me since we mustered in. My mama always wanted me to cut my braid, said it would make things easier on me with the townsfolk. As if people like you would suddenly accept me as an American if I cut my hair. Changing my hair changes nothing, but it does take away the one thing—one thing—that I have left from my blood family."

"By my count, that's two families for you. One who loved ya enough to send ya away, and another that loves ya enough to try to protect ya."

"I am sorry for what you've gone through, Henry, honest."

"Ah, forget it, Tommy-boy. Just keep on feeling sorry for yourself."

Thomas's head ached, but he felt the weight on his chest lift somewhat as he approached the creek. He anticipated Sam's bright smile, his special way of seeing past trouble. The thought of the big man crouched on the bank, messing with a fishing line or jingling the checkers in his huge palm coerced a slight smile from Thomas's face.

Yes, Sam would make it all right. He'd say the war isn't lost. He'd remind Thomas that light action at Chancellorsville was some kind of blessing, maybe God's way of saving him for something bigger. Sam would affirm another chance for the Fourteenth Connecticut on another day. Sam would take the edge off of Thomas's run-in with Henry, too—he had a way.

Thomas bellowed a hello to his friend as he approached. When he didn't hear a return greeting, Thomas shouted his name. Still, there was nothing. Thomas shrugged his shoulders and fought against an unsettling lurch in his stomach as he reached the bank. Sam always fished at sundown.

"Must be in camp," Thomas figured. Something had to have come up—some officer needing him for something. Sam's expansive skill set had proven handy to the brass. He was surely a good man to have around. Thomas decided to head back toward camp where he was sure Sam would be.

He turned to head that way and bumped into a young black boy standing in front of him, his eyes turned to the ground.

"Pardon me," Thomas stepped back. "I didn't see you there."

"Brother Thomas," the boy looked up shyly. "I's comes to talks to you."

"Oh, well, fine." Thomas motioned to the boulders that flanked the creek. "Shall we sit?"

"Name's Josiah," the boy said, sitting awkwardly.

"It's a pleasure to meet you. How do you know my name?"

"Sam, he talks about you's, says your'n his friend," Josiah said.

"Yes, he is my friend. What did you want to talk with me about? Did Sam send you?"

"Im's sorry to tell you's this, but Sam's gone."

"What do you mean gone?" Thomas jumped to his feet, an icy chill plunging through him.

"Some men says...you sees, um, some soldiers talked to them Rebels, and, well, he says no choice buts to go."

"Say again?" Thomas's face reddened.

"Um," the boy was nervous and stood shyly. "Sam's gone away. He said he's, um, thanks for you's."

Thomas didn't hear anything else the boy said. He saw red; his hands bunched into fists as he darted back to camp. His boots barely touched the ground, the speed of his sprint kicking up dust. His mad dash drew a crowd, surprised soldiers intrigued by the sudden, strong, and striking disturbance in camp.

Thomas spied Henry. He didn't slow up, but pummeled into him, knocked them both to the ground. Henry's head pounced against the dirt and his eyes rolled back at the jolt. Thomas straddled him, sat up, and drew his fist back. Before he could land a punch, James and Elias pulled him off. Robert bolted to them.

"Thomas!" Robert removed his brother from the other boys' grasp and held him by his shirt. "What in tarnation are ya doin'?"

"Sam's gone!" Thomas squirmed against his brother's strong grip, motioned his head toward Henry. "His foolhardy games with the Rebs across the creek alerted Sam's master.... Sam's gone."

"You stupid monkey." Henry slowly got up, wiped his mouth. "I didn't say a darn thing to them Rebs about your Negro, but it wouldn't matter none if I had. Those wealthy Southern *gentlemen* over there, the masters, they know their slaves are hiding in our lines. They were gonna come get 'em sooner or later."

"Through an entire army?" Thomas was breathless. "They wouldn't have gotten through. He was safe here...free here."

"That's bull." Henry discarded his cap. "He was hiding from his master. He broke the law."

"President Lincoln declared him free," Elias interrupted.

"That's right, Elias," James declared, "but he can't enforce that law, not yet. We, the army, have to force them by winning the war."

"He's gone now." Henry pointed at Thomas. "Get over it."

"Did you see the look on his face?" Madeline set a plate of biscuits in front of her husband.

"Aye," Joseph nodded, snatching one up and drowning it in honey. "I had no choice but to say no."

"He so wants to join you on a voyage. He doesn't remember much from coming over, but he remembers being with you on your ship."

"It's not safe for him, Maddy."

"That's what I told him." Madeline joined Joseph at the table. "He doesn't want to question you, but he must wonder why."

"Thomas doesn't need to look back or ever go back. We're his family now. It wouldn't do any good for him to see what happens at those ports."

"Is it as awful as it sounds, Joseph?"

"Worse. This last time I saw a father sell his son for six dollars. The boy's screams still haunt me. He was marched up the gangplank of a Peruvian ship."

"What terrible fate will he meet there?"

"Depends if he survives the five-month voyage. Aye, a British mate told me that as many coolies die on their way to Peru as African slaves en route to America and other places. Once they get there, they work hard labor from dawn 'till dark in the guano pits."

"For goodness sakes, Joseph, what in the heavens is guano?"

"It's not from the heavens, Maddy, but from the other place. Guano is bird droppings." He patted her arm while her eyes filled with disgust. "The coolies chip away guano from rocks on these high and jagged cliffs and then push wheelbarrows great distances to depots where the guano is collected and then emptied into waiting ships for transport to Europe."

"What does Europe want with a bunch of bird droppings?"

"They use it to fertilize their farms." Joseph grabbed another biscuit. "My British mate told me it's ah...how did he put it? A profitable enterprise."

"Sounds just like the Confederacy to me," Madeline huffed. "Profiting on the backs of slave labor."

"Well, I heard tell the coolies work more than one hundred hours a week and are whipped if they stop. They don't get much food but some maggot-infested rice and a few bits of meat each day. They live in bamboo shacks at the foot of the hills. Coolie contracts usually last five years, but the coolies themselves don't."

"Sounds like a tale Ms. Stowe could write."

"It's just as bad as slavery here, that's for sure."

"May God protect that poor boy who was boarding that ship."

"Aye, and we'll protect Thomas. He's safe with us. This is his home now."

Thomas had taken a step back gingerly from the door frame, worried that his parents would scold him for eavesdropping. Thomas had lingered in the hall after being sent to bed. He had needed to know why his father forbade him to accompany him on a return trip to China. Now that he had a better idea, Thomas wished he hadn't overheard.

That dreadful feeling came back to Thomas now like a high-balling train. His insides were shaky; there was a jumpiness under his skin that he just couldn't shake. His temper was quick and his mood was dour. Sitting alone by the creek, Thomas simply couldn't summon the energy to renew the fight. The task before him didn't just seem hard, but impossible. How could he go on?

Robert and Elias had offered to accompany him, to provide some company, but Thomas preferred the solitude. The fact was that Sam was gone. Maybe he had gotten safely out and was on his way to Canada. Maybe he could start over there a free man.

Or, maybe, he was captured right away. If so, he'd be whipped, probably killed. If it weren't for his Chinese family placing him on Joseph's ship.... Thomas didn't like to think about it. In fact, up until he became a soldier fighting to free slaves, he hadn't thought much about it at all.

Thomas held his head in his hands as a lonely desperation engulfed him. Henry may have been right about Thomas's good fortune. So what if he had to fight battles in camp or against the judgements of others for his Chinese queue? While he would never know for sure, he was confident now that he was saved from something far worse than whatever this was—and he forgot to be grateful.

The bugler belted out a familiar call.

CHAPTER NINETEEN

"Lee's headed to Pennsylvania, boys! We're gonna meet 'em."

Thomas stopped packing his bed roll. General Lee was headed north?

It wasn't Lee's first time. The Fourteenth Connecticut's first battle had been at Antietam Creek in Sharpsburg, Maryland. That was technically Northern soil, as Maryland was a border state, all but forced to stay with the Union, but the boys in blue knew its residents harbored Southern sympathies. They had witnessed it on the march as farmers yelled at them and spat at their feet as they came through. It hadn't felt like Union territory.

Pennsylvania was a different state altogether. A Rebel march there changed things—changed everything. The blue troops had always been the pursuers; most of the Civil War's battles had been fought on Southern soil. The blue soldiers thought it gave the gray troops a distinct advantage—anyone would fight tooth and nail to protect his home.

The roles were reversed now. This time General Lee pursued the Yankee troops. Whatever his strategy, General Lee knew that a battle won in Northern territory would be war-changing. A Confederate victory in Pennsylvania, mere miles from Washington City, could potentially end the war. Furthermore, a Southern victory meant the continuation of slavery and the end of the United States as one country.

Thomas recognized a familiar sense of urgency within him, a tinge of excitement. When he first heard the bugler, dread had descended, the prospects of another losing contest on the horizon. His mind was filled with the aftertaste of Chancellorsville; his shoulders carried a desolate sag at the disappearance of his friend. Thomas's trudge back to camp had been on weary and tired feet.

Only through God's mercy, Thomas reckoned, could a hopeless situation change direction so quickly. It's exactly what Sam would have said to Thomas if he'd been here. The next opportunity for the Fourteenth Connecticut was already on the way. Thomas intended to find out what happened to his friend, but right now he had a job to do. The Rebs were pushing north toward victory. The time was now. Stopping Lee in Pennsylvania was all Thomas could think about. Teeming with purpose, Thomas was ready to help the army pave the way for freedom for his friend. Perhaps even for a China boy.

Fighting between North and South sparked in a Pennsylvania town called Gettysburg on the first of July. When the Fourteenth Connecticut reached a ridge overlooking the town early on July the second, they received reports of fierce fighting that had ended with blue troops retreating to their location.

The trek to the top had been uphill on a narrow and uneven path, troops passing by a one-story cottage occupied as headquarters of the army's new commander, General George Meade. Thomas wondered if a new commander was a good omen or a bad one. General Hooker hadn't led them to victory, but there was always another general for President Lincoln to replace him with. Thomas bowed his head as he marched, a silent prayer that Meade was the right man for the coming battle. He saluted as his regiment passed a hastily-placed American flag hanging from the cottage roof.

Ordered to keep their accouterments—ammunition and cartridge pouch—on and arms nearby, the regiment fell out into a grassy field. Thomas and Robert followed the pleasant scent of smoking embers to the front, noted brass artillery pieces positioned in a little grove of trees, and sauntered to the edge of the ridge. The Union position took the shape of a fish hook, the straight part beginning where the boys stood on Cemetery Ridge and following along the heights for two miles. It ended just before two bigger, wooded hills.

The brothers halted at a stonework fence and gazed out over Gettysburg's farm field squares and a few houses dotting the landscape. Thomas's stomach danced from being up so high; he placed one worn leather shoe on the stone to steady himself.

"Will this be where we win the war, Robert?"

"I doubt it, Tom." Robert swatted at a bee buzzing near his ear. "Looks like we got whipped again today."

"A lot's riding on this, Robert." Thomas bit down hard. "We've got to beat them this time."

"Why's this time any different?" Robert spat into a patch of grass, just missing his boot.

"Because this is Northern soil." Thomas staggered, the answer seeming obvious. "They get past us, it's a clear path to Washington."

"The ground don't matter, Tom. They pushed our troops back into these hills yesterday, before we got here. I can just picture them over there—" Robert pointed out into the distance, beyond a seminary with a watch tower, to some elevated wooded hills. "They're resting up and they'll hit us again, probably today."

Thomas shrugged; he chose not to pick a fight. The pair rejoined the regiment in the meadow. Robert greeted Fred and William. Thomas veered to a vacant tree stump.

Time etched on, the temperature comfortable for a mid-summer day, a slight warm southern breeze caressing Thomas's face. He closed his eyes and angled his head to better hear the pleasant squawks and clicks of jaybirds and the fast hammering of a woodpecker nearby. He drew in the air around him, listened to the distant thundering of horses' hoof beats, the clink of cooking utensils, voices mingling together.

Thomas bit off a piece of hard tack, the dry biscuit coating his mouth. Grabbing his canteen, he washed it down, water escaping down his chin. He glanced to his right and noted a cemetery, its tall white gravestones reaching skyward.

"Buried in the middle of a battlefield," Thomas uttered aloud.

"What's that you say, Thomas?" Elias took a straight path to him and took a seat on the grass next to him.

"Hello, Elias," Thomas nodded, glad to see him. "Just supposing there will be more to bury up there after today."

"Yep, that's for certain." Elias stretched his legs and propped himself on one elbow. "You ever think about it?"

"Yes," Thomas admitted, "but not too much. I just shoot when the fighting starts. I think I'm more scared of us losing than getting killed. Wouldn't want to live, anyhow, without freeing the slaves." Thomas closed his eyes. "It really matters, I mean, for someone like me, like Sam."

"I know, Thomas, for you, for Sam, for the country."

"I still wonder sometimes about the cause," Thomas admitted. "It seems so clear to me now, but not all the men seem to want it."

"It?"

"Freedom for the slaves. Freedom for me. I mean, I know I'm not a slave, but..."

"But you aren't fully accepted as one of us, as an American, a citizen."

"And I'd like to be."

"Perhaps someday soon, Thomas."

"So, you ever think about it, Elias? Dying, I mean."

"More now." Elias shrugged his shoulders. "I can't keep my promise to Sarah if I get killed."

"Elias—"

"Maybe that's not the worst," Elias continued. "Suppose I take a blow to the leg and the surgeons have to cut it off? I don't want her saddled with a useless invalid."

"You'd never be useless," Thomas protested. "I hate to think on that. Let's win this darn war so you can get home to her."

"Your lips to God's ears, Thomas." Elias lay back on his arms, pulled his cap down over his eyes.

Lost in a trance, Thomas's gaze fixed on Elias as his snores pushed his cap up and down, whistling as it went.

How can he sleep?

Thomas's leg shook. Irritated and nervous, Thomas wanted to get on with it. He was bone tired of being the Chinese Yankee and of the emotional see-saw of the war.

What on earth are the Rebs waiting for?

At four o'clock there were sounds of artillery. It wasn't directly in front of the Fourteenth, but to their left, from the two big hills at the end of the Union line. The company marched in that direction, causing Thomas's pulse to quicken, but the regiment halted after 200 yards. They positioned themselves behind a loosely-constructed stone wall, near the headquarters of division commander General Alexander Hays. Clouds of smoke ascended from the two big hills.

"I can't see the battle," Thomas said to his brother.

"Me neither, but this ground is a-shaking. It's coming our way."

Thomas felt a hard pull on his queue.

"Hey, China boy, ya got your dander up again?"

Thomas squeezed his eyes shut and yanked his head forward to free himself from the strong tug.

"Henry!" Thomas fought back the sting in his eyes as several strands of hair pulled loose. "What do you think you're doing?"

"Oh, me and James are bored here waiting for the battle." Henry smirked. "We knew you'd be chomping at the bit, jumping around like a little yellow monkey, so we came to have a look-see."

Thomas drew a deep breath. It didn't matter that Thomas had proven he could fight. It always came back to his being Chinese.

Robert pushed Henry down the ridge. Other soldiers came and

grabbed Henry, too, and got him out of the way.

"Hey, just passing time, Tommy. Can't take a joke, eh?" Henry called. "Or maybe it's time to stop foolin' around. You wanna finish what ya started in camp? Fight me on account of that Negro?"

A storm of anger grew in Thomas's chest. He wanted to remind Henry that it was he who had started the fight one year ago, right after they joined up, but he said nothing. He refused to have another public conniption fit. Thomas's hand went to the back of his head. He felt around where the pain was and found a tiny barren spot. It wasn't big, probably not noticeable under his cap, but—joke or not—it hurt just the same.

CHAPTER TWENTY

Thomas awoke on the ground the next day, July 3, the day before Independence Day. The regiment passed the night behind the stone wall, using their knapsacks as pillows, muskets in hand. Sleep had been difficult to come by as the earth shook, Confederate cannons firing long into the night as Federal artillery matched them blast for blast.

Sleep had mostly eluded Thomas. His mind lost in thought, he re-braided his queue through the night. He used his sweaty palm to make the sides lay flat, used cowhide to tie the knot in the back of his head, and braided it. He crossed one thin set of strands over another, found it imperfect each time, and unwound it. Lost in the motions and in thought about Henry's antics, Thomas knew with certainty that he'd never chop it off. He would be an American on his terms, and as himself.

212 | Stacie Haas

The morning dawned beautifully, the pale blue sky visible behind swaths of white streaks, like God fanned white feathers across it. Men stretched their limbs and grinded coffee beans as messengers carried orders on horseback and wagons brought supplies. The army's business carried on as booms of war thudded in the distance. The sounds came from the right of the Fourteenth Connecticut's position, nearly behind them, on the "hook" of the Union position, a ridge called Culps Hill.

Despite the inaction of the Fourteenth Connecticut the day before, the officers reported fierce fighting between the Yankees and Rebels. The Confederate troops had threatened to break through a local peach orchard, a boulder-strewn patch called Devil's Den, and the Round Tops, wooded hills at the flank of the Union line.

Thomas was relieved to learn that the Union position on Cemetery Ridge remained intact, stories of heroism and valor coming in from the Round Tops, the boys in gray retreating back across the field, again positioned on the opposite ridge with the seminary on it.

Thomas prayed for action. He didn't want another day and night like yesterday and definitely not another battle like Chancellorsville. He'd grown tired of sitting around, waiting, passing more hours thinking about things he shouldn't. He looked out to the cemetery again, recalled his talk with Elias, and hoped Sam had made it to his destination safely.

Orders came in just after sunrise for several companies of the Fourteenth Connecticut to man the skirmish line, a row of troops who went ahead of the main body, their mission to harass the Confederate skirmishers. Enemy officer tassels and raised Rebel heads were their targets.

Thomas jumped. He found a lieutenant and approached without hesitation.

"Sir, Thomas Beck. I volunteer to man the line."

"You're in F Company, right soldier?"

"Yes, sir. Beg your pardon, sir, but I'm ready to go."

"I won't stop you, boy." The lieutenant had looked Thomas over and shrugged.

"Are you a skirmisher?" Elias approached from behind Thomas, who was silently celebrating.

"Yes," Thomas nodded. "Have to do something. Tired of sitting here."

"I'll come, too."

The boys crawled across the wheat field on their bellies, creeping through the rough crops, their guns heavy and the ground scratchy. All was quiet save for the muffled, earthy sounds of other men scuffling though the stalks and grasses. No one dared to speak and make a comrade raise his head to answer their call.

The pair reached a wood rail fence, kept their heads down, and fanned out to man a post about twelve feet apart. Thomas prepped his weapon but grew impatient with the lack of clear targets as time wore on.

Shots and smoke drew his eyes to the right, to a massive two-story brick barn, the biggest Thomas had ever seen. It had a sloped earthen roadway to allow horses to pull a wagon right up to the second floor. Thomas thought that clever and wondered if his father had considered that.

The thought vanished when Thomas noted sinister-looking rifle muzzles protruding from the barn's windows and slits. Thomas shuddered and stiffened his resolve to stay quiet, to avoid their aim at his spot. Blue troops raced to the barn, bayonets fixed.

"Go get 'em, boys," Thomas whispered. "Clear them out."

Thomas veered his eyes to Elias and calmed the butterflies as he waited for Elias to notice. When he finally did, Elias cocked his head. Thomas followed his friend's nod across the field to a Confederate officer in a tall gray hat, behind the Rebel skirmishers, only half hidden by a tree trunk. Thomas smiled and blinked understanding to Elias.

From his stomach, Elias sighted his gun, the barrel under the fence's bottom rail. He pulled the trigger.

The shot missed! Elias ducked the return fire, the Rebs aiming at the smoke ascending from his gun.

Bells exploded in Thomas's head, a loud clanging in his ears, the fear muzzling his voice. *Wait Elias*, Thomas urged him in his heart. *Just a bit 'till your gun smoke is gone. Please wait.*

Elias rose to one knee, his head visible under the top fence rail. He primed his weapon, took careful aim, and pulled the trigger.

Thomas's breath caught. He squeezed his eyes shut, opened them to see the Rebel clasp his chest and fall backwards. Thomas stifled a celebratory yell, shot a glance at Elias, a rush of affection warming his body.

Elias's face changed. His lips dropped apart and a gray cloudiness filled his eyes.

"No!" Thomas shouted, the pitch in his voice elevating to a desperate cry. He crawled as fast as he could to find his friend slumped over the fence. Panic gripping him, Thomas pulled Elias back from the rail, the weight forcing Thomas flat on his back, his friend on top of him, the pair making a human size impression in the wheat field. The commotion revealed their position to the sharpshooters and bullets flew across their bodies.

Soldiers from the Fourteenth, who had been watching from their reserve position on the Emmitsburg Road, clambered to them as fast as they could crawl, six men taking up arms on the ground where the pair had been. The soldiers loosed a barrage of masking fire to cover the Yankees pulling Thomas and Elias back to the ridge.

Elias's body was still, his eyes fixed open, as if seeing something startling in the heavens above. He lie on top of Thomas, who refused to let go. Thomas gagged, choking on his uniform collar, as men pulled at the fabric on his shoulders. He scrambled with his feet, an attempt to help the men whose shoulders and backs screamed in protest, danger forbidding them from standing up straight.

"Elias." Thomas sobbed once they were behind the stone wall again. Tears streamed down his face. Thomas strained his abdominals to sit himself up, felt Elias's body with his hands and searched for a clue but found nothing. Something warm and wet slid down Thomas's neck. He pushed Elias forward to see a horrendous patch of blood on the lower right side of Elias's head.

A soldier mumbled something about fetching help, but Thomas didn't hear him. He moaned, rocked Elias back and forth, and soothed him like a mother comforts her infant. As his arms held Elias tight, Thomas's chest compressed from a cannon's weight of pain and grief. He gasped for air.

Anger and hatred, sadness and hopelessness gripped Thomas as he shook, his shoulders heaving through heavy sobs. The war came back in flashes now—leaving his homestead, the strains with Robert, the wrenching struggles with Henry, Sam's leaving, every strange look and averted eye. The officer's words at the recruiting station—"stop a bullet as good as a white man"—rang in his ears like a loud, clanging gong. Now he'd lost his first real friend.

CHAPTER TWENTY-ONE

The Bliss family of Gettysburg owned the big barn that Thomas saw from the skirmish line. For more than a day, troops from New York, Delaware, Pennsylvania, and New Jersey had fought to wrestle the buildings from the Rebels and prevent their sharpshooters from killing blue troops on Cemetery Ridge. From his forward position early that morning, Thomas had watched the Twelfth New Jersey attack it. They captured many Confederate prisoners, but it had been too perilous a position to hold.

General Hays, tired of the sharpshooters picking off his men, summoned the Fourteenth Connecticut. The bugle call lifted Thomas's head, his face wet with tears. Men swallowed down their breakfasts and coffee, scrambled into formation. General Hays ordered the Fourteenth to take the Bliss buildings "to stay."

With a tender squeeze, Thomas let Elias go, prayed for his friend's soul, and nodded to the burial detail. A sting rose in Thomas's nose as they tended to his friend. He felt a strong hand on his shoulder.

"Thomas." Robert's eyes were soft. "Them sharpshooters have killed the last one of us if we have anything to say about it."

"How did you know?" Thomas wiped his eyes.

"That shot was near the back of his head—only a sharpshooter in them blasted barn windows could make that shot."

"For Elias." Thomas breathed in the sadness, felt it envelop and strengthen him.

"For Elias," Robert repeated.

The Fourteenth filed off the ridge, down the slope, and marched over the Emmitsburg Road, not far from where Elias was shot. They approached a field, fire from gray troops intensifying, orders to break ranks. The troops scattered and ran. Thomas started off as fast as his legs would carry him, his breath labored. James fell from a gunshot wound with an awful scream.

Thomas yearned to help, but there was no time, Captain Moore of his Company F was barking orders to get to the barn...now!

The troops sprinted to the barn's exterior stone wall, taking advantage of the momentary protection it offered. The Confederates in the barn retreated in haste at their first view of the Fourteenth's furious approach. The Rebs leveled parting shots as they left.

Captain Moore went into the barn first and sixty men of the Fourteenth followed. Thomas dropped to the barn floor, gunfire smoke and hay dust choking him. He scrambled to an open window slit and carefully rose to peer through it.

"Where'd you go, graybacks?" Thomas asked aloud.

Rebel troops took cover in the Bliss family house, its white frame about 50 yards to the northeast. Other Rebs filtered out into an orchard.

Artillery fire from Seminary Ridge was hot, the shots landing in the sides of the barn, its walls shaking from the impact. Thomas coughed and spat, forcing the dirt-filled sputum out of his throat. He remembered the window and lowered his head. He refused to be a target for a lucky Minnie ball.

"We're stuck, Tom!" Robert had crawled to his brother. He panted, sweat dripping from his forehead. "We haven't got enough men to charge and clear the Rebs out of the house. Ain't no wonder none of our troops could hold this wicked barn."

Thomas started to respond, an explosion above the brothers interrupting him. Thomas covered his head with his arms to protect himself from the falling debris.

General Hays had said they were to hold the buildings at all costs. That suited Thomas. He wasn't about to give it back to the troops who'd killed Elias. Danger or not, he wasn't leaving. He ducked again, a piece of wood splintering off from a rafter, just missing his head.

Thomas rose up to get a better look, his pulse quickening at what he saw.

"Robert! The rest of the Fourteenth—here they come!" He slapped his brother's back.

"Good, good." Robert wiped his brow. "Maybe now we've got a chance."

The brothers watched as best they could as the four remaining companies of the Fourteenth Connecticut approached the Bliss buildings. Thomas winced as he saw many cut down by rifle fire from the house and orchard, and let out his breath when many reached the house, some joining them in the barn.

Thick, gray smoke choked the men and made it hard to see in front of them. Abandoned chickens clucked and whined as they flitted about, their noise grating on Thomas's nerves as he focused on shielding himself from Confederate shell blasts.

Despite the danger, Thomas risked another peer through the window. He noticed a Rebel lieutenant near a bush alongside the house. He threaded his rifle into the slit's narrow opening.

"For Elias," he whispered. Thomas pulled the trigger and felt a penetrating jolt as the shot left the barrel, a hopeless desperation filling him. The Rebel officer fell backwards. Thomas wiped his watering eyes, as much from smoke as sadness at what he'd felt compelled to do.

Only in war, Thomas thought.

Orders came to spread out and dismantle stacks of hay piled up against the barn's outer edges. A soldier on horseback had carried orders from General Hays to torch the barn and house.

Thomas pulled the straw and spread it out on his hands and knees. He liked the thought of burning the barn and forced away any regret for the farmer who built it. If the Yankees couldn't hold it—and hundreds of blue troops had already tried—they had to make sure the Rebs didn't get it back.

The regiment worked to evacuate the wounded as the flames ignited. Thomas and Robert ran to a soldier needing to be carried, shot through the stomach. Robert lifted the man up from his shoulders; Thomas grabbed his left leg. Henry had hold of the soldier's right one.

Thomas and Henry staggered backwards toward Cemetery Ridge when a rifle shot flew past them. It missed, but fury engulfed Thomas. He let go of the injured soldier's leg and darted in the direction of the shot.

"Thomas, no!" Robert yelled.

He advanced, musket fixed forward,and searched for the Reb's hiding spot. Thomas tripped over a stone in the grass and fell hard with a heavy thump. His body felt heavy as he rolled over, his head aching as he opened his eyes. A grayback stood above him, his bayonet glinting in the sunlight, ready to pierce Thomas's chest.

Thomas steeled himself for the impact, clamped his eyes down tight. A heavy object landed on his chest and forced a loud groan to escape from his mouth.

Thomas couldn't breathe due to the Reb on top of him. He screamed and strained his muscles to push him off, saw blood on the soldier's chest. Thomas lifted his head and saw smoke from the barrel of Henry's gun. Thomas caught Henry's eye and held his gaze.

"You're welcome, China boy." Henry gave him a hearty nod.

Thomas pushed the dead Rebel off of him and ran back to the injured man. He grunted aloud, panting as he and Henry resumed their backwards climb to safety, their comrade's legs once again in their grasp. When they reached a flat knoll in the earth, Robert motioned for them to rest a bit and readjust. Thomas had a perfect view of orange flames rising from the detested barn, dark gray clouds of smoke billowing in the sky.

CHAPTER TWENTY-TWO

Thomas's eyes were transfixed on the gray smoke clouds, the Bliss buildings nearly gone by the time the Fourteenth Connecticut returned to the ridge. He sat on the grass behind the stone wall and propped himself up against a wagon's wheel, its supply days over, half its bed blown off by an artillery shell.

Thomas searched for some emotion as he watched the remnants of the buildings smolder. He felt no relief, no satisfaction—only a profound exhaustion. The morning's events crushed Thomas, weighed him down. Elias's loss sat on his chest like a boulder.

It was just after 12 o'clock. Ninety-degree temperatures had settled on the ridge, the hot sun beat down, the stink of sweat, blood, and ash clinging to Thomas like a testy burr. He considered finding a canteen, something to wash the grime off, but it felt like too much work. Besides, the muck on the outside of Thomas's body mirrored the inside—covered by a thick film of weariness and sadness. He didn't like the feeling, but somehow he'd earned it, and for the moment, he owned it.

The fighting at Gettysburg had lasted two straight days, the battle hard, the losses mounting. After waging fierce battles against both flanks of the Union army, many officers on Cemetery Ridge assumed General Lee would need to rest and regroup before resuming the battle on a large scale.

Thomas jumped. The unmistakable thunder and shaking earth of artillery fire woke him from a deep sleep. He grabbed his musket, looking for the battle.

"Whoa there, China boy!" Henry called out. "Ain't no targets yet. They're gonna try to clear us off this ridge with them wretched guns first."

It could have been the sleep in Thomas's eyes or the smoke that again filled the air, but Thomas could have sworn that Sam passed in front of him. Thomas rubbed his eyes and squinted to see better, but he was gone. It was just Henry, who appeared to wink at him.

Thomas shook his head.

What is happening to me? There's no way Sam is here or that

Henry of all people is winking at me. Well, maybe that really happened. The same guy who beat me during my first days of camp on account of my being Chinese, who pulled my queue just hours ago, just saved my life. Maybe he does remember my helping him down Marye's Heights at Fredericksburg....

Thomas suppressed the swirling questions in his brain, knowing no answers would come now. Henry was right. The barrage could go on for hours. Thomas couldn't help but notice that the artillery seemed concentrated on their position, about two hundred feet north of a copse of oak trees on the ridge. Thomas scanned the area for a safer spot to wait it out, but, finding nothing, crouched down by the wagon wheel.

Shrieking down from a blast behind him, Thomas wished he knew where Robert was. It'd be a comfort to have him nearby, but he remembered that his brother had been granted permission to find the field hospital and inquire about James and other wounded men from the Fourteenth.

Thomas's shoulders ached, the constant tightening at his neck uncomfortable, each explosion causing him to clench. He brushed debris from his cap and soot from his eyes. How much longer could this go on? Did the Rebs have an endless supply of cannon balls?

Thomas pinched his nose shut, squeezed his eyes tight so they'd water. The sky was raining black ash, tiny sulfur particles that blackened faces, stuck to lips, and assaulted tongues. Thomas grabbed some hard tack from inside his coat—at least the dry cracker coated his mouth with something less offensive than the acrid, bitter taste of war. But now he needed water to wash it down.

He surveyed the ridge: dead horses, splintered wagons and barrels, craters in the earth, but no canteen. It was a gruesome truth, but sometimes a dead comrade's last contribution to the war effort was his abandoned gun or canteen to another soldier.

Finding no water, Thomas spat the remnants of his biscuit and wiped his mouth with his sleeve. He settled down near the wagon wheel again and held onto its spokes, the strong, smooth wood reassuring as the earth shook.

The barrage continued for two full hours, each minute loud and jarring. Thomas was wiping sweat and grime from his face when he realized the pounding in his ears had stopped. He glanced up to see through the dissipating smoke that other soldiers started to rise, conversations resuming now that they could be heard.

Soldiers gathered at the stone wall so Thomas stood, fire

screaming in his limbs from crouching so long. He ambled like an old man to the edge of the ridge, stretching his legs as he went, and knelt down on one knee behind the rocks. He sighted his musket.

Stepping out of the trees from Seminary Ridge were gray troops, stretched over a mile, marching his way, three rows deep. What a marvelous sight! Grand to behold, the soldiers appeared to be holding a grand review for Confederate President Jefferson Davis instead of making a charge. Although Thomas couldn't make out their flags or hear their patriotic songs, he could almost hear their raised voices for Virginia, for Tennessee, for North Carolina and Alabama, and for Texas.

Thomas looked down the ridge, his eyes following the rolling slope and across the mile of farm fields and grasses to the Army of Northern Virginia. He noted the fence at the Emmitsburg Road, where he and Elias had been skirmishers, noted the embers of what was once the Bliss family homestead. He noted the big seminary on the opposite ridge, its white cupola visible from his spot.

The soldiers marching toward him would soon give heated battle, but now a strange calm descended, the war happening in slow motion, a lazy dream unfolding. Thomas stared as they came closer, almost admired them.

They are Americans like us, Thomas thought, *fighting for their way of life. It's unfortunate that slavery has be a part of it.*

Thomas's chest tightened, a keen reminder of Elias. Those boys in gray had killed his best friend. He felt immense and penetrating pain, but no hatred for those boys over there. He loathed slavery, not the soldiers; slavery was the enemy. *We're supposed to be America, land of the free.*

"Those boys are worthy of a better cause." Robert knelt down beside Thomas.

Thomas clutched his brother and gathered him in tight. Robert patted his brother's back, held his strong hand there and left an impression on Thomas's back.

"James?" Thomas asked, a hopeful look in his black eyes.

Robert shook his head no. Sadness punched Thomas again in the gut.

"Look at all the colors." Robert was referring to the regimental flags, each sewn and adorned with personal markers. Flags were a source of tremendous pride; color bearers who carried flags in battle were unarmed and stood strong in the face of oncoming fire. They never dared retreat for the flag marked a regiment's position in battle, beaconed hope for weary troops. No soldier on either side wanted to see their flag fall—its rips and tatters represented every battle fought and every life lost.

"How many do you think there are?" Thomas followed his brother's arm, his pointer finger moving up and down as he counted.

"Too many to tell, Tom, but ya know there are hundreds, thousands of soldiers behind every one of them." There were, in fact, more than twelve thousand Rebels marching their way.

The Fourteenth Connecticut numbered somewhat less than one hundred men, having lost half their strength since arriving from Gettysburg, down from over one thousand when they mustered into service less than a year before. A small part of General Winfield Hancock's Second Corps, the Fourteenth Connecticut stood in the middle of a long line of Yankee troops that held the ridges this side of town. Thomas turned his head to see behind him and noted troops in reserve, but the line looked too thin to stand against that many enemy troops.

At least we have the heights this time, Thomas figured. *It's their turn to attack uphill.*

General Hays approached and led the men in a drill review as the gray wave inched closer. The men followed orders, knowing the general was keeping them occupied—and patient.

"Now boys, look out; you will see some fun in short order," the commander shouted.

Thomas's nerves pricked his insides as he started to make out details on the flags, glints of sunlight on the Rebel bayonets. He cringed as the Yankee artillery tore a hole in part of the Confederate line, men disappearing in an instant. The soldiers closed up, kept coming, and approached the Emmitsburg Road. More shells exploded on them, the fence a good target, the cannon fire disrupting their organized approach.

"Wait, boys," the general shouted. "Preserve your ammunition. Don't fire until you see the whites of their eyes."

Thomas shivered. He steeled himself for the fight, his will strong. He bowed his head, prayed for strength, for the souls about to be lost. Before he finished, he asked that the day's victory rest on freedom's side.

"Here we go, Robert." Thomas tapped his brother's shoulder and realized his dream to fight alongside his brother had come true more than once.

"I'm glad you're here, Tom. Ya make one heck of a soldier."

"Beck boys always do."

The gray-clad troops continued their approach, some changing direction and then veering back toward the second corps, closing up and coming still. Thomas's finger tapped the trigger, ready to fire.

"Just a little more," Thomas whispered. "Keep coming."

An enemy brigade approached, and the pounding in Thomas's heart grew furious.

"Hold your fire, boys," General Hays shouted. "Wait—"

Just two hundred yards away now, the brigade of Johnnies quickened their pace. Thomas itched, ready to shoot. His heart leaped when he heard a raucous yell from the general.

"Now, boys! Pour it into 'em!"

The men of the Fourteenth Connecticut rose on one knee and together let loose a torrent of lead. The gunfire swallowed up the Rebs in an immense cloud of dust. When it cleared, the men in front of him had all but disappeared. Thomas had no time to mull over that for another set of troops approached just behind. Thomas crouched lower behind the stone fence, enemy fire interrupting his process of reloading and shooting, but he persisted.

Several boys fell with awful screams, but Thomas averted his eyes; he wouldn't watch more of his comrades die. After every shot, he made sure Robert knelt beside him, then pulled his rammer out to reload, aim, and fire.

The graybacks kept coming. Wave after endless wave came upon them. The Fourteenth Connecticut struggled to hold their line. The Rebs were right in front of them now—no more time to load and shoot. They were too close!

A Confederate general leapt over their stone fence, leading his boys, tried to turn a federal cannon on its own troops. Thomas and Robert screamed and joined Henry and Fred and William leaping over the wall. They lunged to meet the gray mass.

Thomas grabbed one from behind, pulled him to the ground, and smacked him in the face. The pain tore through Thomas's hand, but he kept flailing. Another Reb grabbed Thomas, the butt of his weapon striking him with brutal force. Thomas landed hard, but he rose and kicked the soldier in the shin. Another came, his bayonet swinging, but Thomas ducked, pulling the soldier's legs out from under him.

Drenched in sweat, Thomas panted as salty droplets fell from his nose. Confederate soldiers were corralled as prisoners on his left, reserve troops filing in, so he ran to the right where more gray and blue troops fought with their hands.

He sprinted there, seeing a redhead seize a battle flag from a Tennessee regiment. Thomas recognized Henry and called out to him. Henry noted Thomas and raised the flag higher, the two celebrating together with boisterous yells.

Thomas sprinted to him, eager to share his victory. A Rebel officer lying on the ground near Henry drew his pistol and cocked the hammer.

"Henry," Thomas yelled. "Watch out!"

Henry shot Thomas a confused look and yelped when Thomas threw his body into him and tackled him to the ground. The Reb's shot went off but missed his target. Henry sat up, looked Thomas in the eye, and motioned to his left.

"The flag."

Thomas lunged across Henry's body, scrambled to retrieve it. He pulled his legs under him and managed to stand the heavy wood pole upright and rise. The Rebel soldier on the ground, whose first shot missed, cocked his revolver again. This time his bullet found a new target.

CHAPTER TWENTY-THREE

Thomas felt an endless pounding in his head, a rapid succession of musket fire and cannon shells, the deafening noise growing louder as he labored to breathe. Bursts of pain radiated from his right shoulder, where the Confederate bullet had lodged into his flesh.

Thomas came slowly awake to the din of clinking medical instruments, a scent both sweet and metallic, and moaning and groaning men. And something else, too, the most pleasant sound he'd heard in a long time—a woman's voice. She was speaking familiar words, verses from the Bible, the book of Jeremiah...wait!

"Mama?" Thomas's voice cracked as he strained to open his eyes and lift his aching head.

"I'm here, my son." Madeline reached out to smooth her son's hair.

"How did you get here?" Thomas managed.

"Aye, your brother sent word." Thomas shot up at the sound of his father's voice. "Oh, now, don't you go straining yourself. The surgeons took that bullet out and sewed you up all fancy-like with a piece of thread like your Mama uses in her sewing kit. It's the darnedest thing."

"Wait, Pa, where is here? Where are we? The battle...."

"Aye, settle down, my boy. You are in an army hospital in Pennsylvania. Your brother managed to save the life of an officer after you fell wounded. After the Confederates retreated, Robert asked him for help getting word to us.. The officer, an adjutant, sent us a message over a wire, something called a telegraph. The message went to the postmaster in Hartford and he dispatched a messenger to the homestead. We got the wire read to us before we'd even heard of a battle happening at Gettysburg."

Joseph patted Thomas's arm and Madeline picked up the story.

"We boarded a train the next day from Hartford. It took just five days for us to get here by the rail ways. One of the conductors told us we came more than 300 miles."

"Mama, you spent five full days on a train?"

"Nothing could have kept me from you. I worried every minute on the journey, but not about the train. About you, my son."

"And the battle? It got too close for muskets. I didn't even have time to fix my bayonet. I grabbed a Rebel flag, and—"

"You were shot in the shoulder," Joseph finished Thomas's sentence, "but the surgeons took it out, as I said. You lost a lot of blood and you've been weak, but they say you'll be fine."

"And the battle? We won?"

"Aye, before they went back on the march, your friend, Henry, left this with the surgeon for you." Joseph grabbed a newspaper from a table beside Thomas's cot. *The Philadelphia Inquirer* headline said, "Victory! Waterloo Eclipsed!"

Joseph handed his wife the newspaper with a look that implored her to read it to Thomas.

Henry left me a newspaper? Henry visited me here at the hospital?

Thomas listened intently as his mama read the report. The momentous battle of Gettysburg had ended not long after Thomas fell wounded. His Second Corps had repulsed General Lee's attack—what was now being called Pickett's Charge, named for Confederate Major General George Pickett—and defended their position on the high ground. The depleted troops of Lee's

Army of Northern Virginia had been forced to retreat to the immediate safety of southern territory.

Success at Gettysburg combined with Union General Ulysses S. Grant's siege of Vicksburg, Mississippi, in another theater of the war on July 4 had given the North cause for great celebration on Independence Day. The reporter's reference to Napoleon's Battle of Waterloo predicted the decline of the South and the Confederacy's high water mark—the point in which it could no longer sustain itself. Victory for the North, in the reporter's humble opinion at least, was a simple matter of time.

Thomas knelt down on one knee, reached down to touch the cool grass where the blood of the fallen had soaked the earth. He swiped his hand gently across the blades, soft across the palm of his hand, even in chilly November. With a heavy heart, he recalled Elias, who fell not far from his spot. He thought of James, cut down by musket fire.

Thomas blew fog from his breath and watched the cloud rise to the heavens, memories scrolling through his mind: Henry saving him from a Rebel bayonet; Thomas returning the favor as Henry guarded the prize of the Tennessee battle flag; the bullet that tore through his shoulder.

Thomas stood with a start and shook the thoughts from his head. There would be no more of that. He intended to hold himself together today for the dedication of the cemetery. He was a veteran—a survivor—of the three-day battle of Gettysburg. There were fifty thousand men on both sides who could not be here, who lost their lives on this field just three months ago. Thomas would be strong in their honor.

Ambling across the battlefield, Thomas was breathing hard trying to maintain a healthy pace in the thin air. Thomas had recovered from his shoulder wound and endured months at the convalescent camp, regaining full movement and strength in his arm. Still, his legs hadn't been stretched out in a long while; He was no longer used to the exertion of the march. He focused on that, on the burn in his legs, and not the lump in his throat as he approached the crowd.

Thomas would soon be back in the company of his brother and the Fourteenth. He was grateful for the furlough, for permission to be here on this important day. But once it was over, he'd board a train bound for Brandy Station to meet up with his friends. He'd be going home.

"For consider, my friends, what would have been the consequences to the country, to yourselves, and to all you hold dear, if those who sleep beneath our feet, and their gallant comrades who survive to serve their country on other fields of danger, had failed in their duty on those memorable days...."

Thomas felt his composure weakening. He figured it was the famous orator, Edward Everett, who was speaking, his reputation as a speechmaker clearly earned. What elegant words about something so terrible!

Thomas worked his way through the crowd. His uniform seemed to grant him a friendly parting, men in suits making way for him. Thomas wanted a place up front when President Lincoln took the stage. Thomas longed to hear what the president had to say.

The voices hushed in one great, silent wave when the black hat appeared on the platform.

"Four score and seven years ago our fathers brought forth on this continent, a new nation, conceived in Liberty, and dedicated to the proposition that all men are created equal.

Now we are engaged in a great civil war, testing whether that nation, or any nation so conceived and dedicated, can long endure. We are met on a great battle-field of that war. We have come to dedicate a portion of that field, as a final resting place for those who here gave their lives that that nation might live. It is altogether fitting and proper that we should do this.

But, in a larger sense, we can not dedicate – we can not consecrate – we can not hallow – this ground. The brave men, living and dead, who struggled here, have consecrated it, far above our poor power to add or detract.

The world will little note, nor long remember what we say here, but it can never forget what they did here.

It is for us the living, rather, to be dedicated here to the unfinished work which they who fought here have thus far so nobly advanced.

It is rather for us to be here dedicated to the great task remaining before us -- that from these honored dead we take increased devotion to that cause for which they gave the last full measure of devotion – that we here highly resolve that these dead shall not have died in vain – that this nation, under God, shall have a new birth of freedom – and that government of the people, by the people, for the people, shall not perish from the earth."

Thomas let the words sink in. There was still work to be done because while freedom had advanced, it had not yet been won. He felt a warm, strong hand on his shoulder.

"Thomas." Sam opened his arms.

"Sam!" Thomas ran into them and squeezed hard. Despite a creeping embarrassment, tears welled in his eyes as he pulled back. "Am I seeing things?"

"Not 'less I am, too." Sam's smile was broad and wide.

"Where did you go? I was lost without...I mean, I missed you something awful."

"I's hads to go, Thomas." Sam bowed his head. "We's was worried about getting's captured and couldn't stays and wait for it. We heards tell of some officers letting us be soldiers and so set off lookin' for 'em. I's sorry for it, Thomas, but I had to give's it a go. You's understanding?"

"I do understand." Thomas knew the fear of being sidelined, of needing to be part of a war whose outcome mattered to everyone. "So, are you a soldier?"

"Nah, not's yet. But Sam's works for the army on what you's call it? Burial detail. It's not pretty work, but Sam's earn wages. First time for that. I's been here, in this here state of 'Vania, for some time."

"Were you here during the battle, in July?"

Sam nodded his head.

"I saw you, or at least I thought I did. I wish I could have trusted it; it would have helped. Elias, he was killed."

"I's sorry, Thomas. So many men died here—too many for old Sam's to count. You's ought to be proud. All these Northern boys fighting so I's can be free."

"So all of us can, Sam."

Thomas approached the blue troops in a makeshift camp, a ball of energy tight in his gut.

"...and there was Private Beck, pigtail and all, the only Chinese in the Army of the Potomac."

Henry's toothy smile was wide, the reporter on one knee, scribing notes from their exchange. Thomas stepped forward and noted the rolled copy of *Harper's Weekly* tucked inside the man's pocket. He had a spare pencil stuck between his ear and his cap.

"And here he is now, my friend, Tommy." Henry stepped around the reporter and reached his hand to Thomas, who took it. "Lookee here, boys, old Tommy-boy is back."

A blue mass encircled him, hearty smiles and pats on the back. One big hand remained in place, and Thomas knew instantly to whom it belonged. He checked an excited outburst and turned slowly to face his brother. He glanced skyward and the infectious smile tore through him and ruined his resolve. His laugh bellowed even as it was buried in the thickness of his brother's chest.

"Hey, now, careful now big brother." Thomas's laugh simmered to a chuckle. "The surgeons worked hard to fix me up—don't you go messing it up again."

"Oh, right." Robert gently pushed his brother back from his grasp. "Sorry."

"I'm just fooling, Robert." Thomas shoved him. "I'm good as new."

"Well, that's mighty fine 'cause there's lots of folks here to speak with ya."

"How's that, Robert?" He turned serious. "What's all this about?"

The pair turned as the reporter approached.

"So you are the one everybody's talking about," the reporter said matter-of-factly. "The only Chinese in the army, the first corporal."

"The first what?" Thomas's confusion was all over his face.

The crowd parted as Colonel Morris led a trail of officers toward them.

"Private Beck!"

"Sir." Thomas stepped forward and saluted.

"Know ye: That reposing special trust and confidence in the patriotism, valor, fidelity, and abilities of Private Thomas Beck, I do hereby appoint him Corporal in Company F in the 14th Regiment of Connecticut Volunteers in the service of the United States, to rank as such from this day, one thousand eight hundred and sixty-three."

Thomas stiffened his body as Colonel Morris spoke. To others, he stood as a perfect soldier, but Thomas guarded against a fall as his insides puddled and threatened to go soft.

"He is therefore carefully and diligently to discharge the duty of corporal by doing and performing all things thereunto belong. And I do strictly charge and require all soldiers under this command to be obedient to his orders as corporal."

Stand tall, Thomas ordered himself. *Don't fidget.*

"And he is to observe and follow such orders and direction from time to time as he shall receive from me or the future commanding officer of the regiment, or other superior officers and non-commissioned officers set over him according to the rules and discipline of war."

Colonel Morris offered his hand. Thomas took it.

"Congratulations, Corporal."

Whoops and hollers filled the air. Thomas felt an immense

pride and joy as the regiment pulled him from his feet. Henry's shoulders were strong beneath Thomas as he looked down over his company. It was a view Thomas never could have imagined just one year ago.

After a rendition of "He's a Jolly Good Fellow" and several rounds of hurrahs, Thomas's feet finally touched ground again. He came face to face with Henry.

"Bully for ya, Tommy-boy." Henry nodded to Thomas.

"Thank you, Henry. I mean, thank you for saving my life."

"Hey, what are friends for?" Henry slapped Thomas's good shoulder. "Don't think it gets you out of camp duties...we'll be building us another log hut here soon. This cold is gettin' harsh."

"A hut for you and me?"

"Well, at least us, anyways. Probably gonna get some new fellas joining us on account of Elias and James, but at least ya and me, we're still here together."

"Together," Thomas repeated.

"'Till the end, China boy." Henry reached behind Thomas and jostled his *queue* playfully. "Oh, shoot, pardon me." Henry took one giant step back.

"Henry, what are you—"

"Sir, I mean." Henry saluted. "Corporal, sir!"

Henry winked and made way for the reporter who had returned. Thomas shook his head, dizzy with joy and confusion and shock.

"What's it like to be first?" the reporter asked, continuing his line of questioning without missing a beat.

"It's a privilege," Thomas answered without hesitation, "to help spread freedom in America."

"Freedom for the slaves?"

"No," Thomas considered. "Freedom for all of us."

AUTHOR'S NOTE

The character of Thomas Beck is based on a real-life Chinese Yankee, Joseph Pierce, who was mustered in with the Fourteenth Regiment, Connecticut Volunteer Infantry in July of 1862, after the Civil War had been raging between North and South for one year. On his enlistment papers, Joseph listed his hometown as Canton, China, his occupation as a farmer, and his age as 21. Joseph was promoted to Corporal in November 1863. He survived to see the North's victory in April, 1865, and the freeing of the slaves when the Thirteenth Amendment to the U.S. Constitution was ratified on December 6, 1865. Joseph became a naturalized citizen in 1866 under an act passed by Congress during the war, which promised citizenship to any honorably discharged veteran upon his petition.

While the history of how Joseph came to America isn't entirely clear, we know that he journeyed to America as a young boy on the ship of Amos Peck, a sea captain. Some histories suggest that he was adrift in the South China Sea and picked up by Peck; other histories suggest that Joseph's father sold him into slavery for the price of six dollars because he was desperate for money to feed his starving family.

While no evidence exists to prove that Joseph was saved from a coolie contract, it is a fact that these contracts of indentured servitude were one way that the Chinese could escape harsh living conditions in China under the rule of the Qing Dynasty. A coolie contract offered many the opportunity to escape their suffering and begin again in a different land—not unlike Europeans in the 17th century who saw indentured servitude as their path to the New World and a better life. It was under the Qing Dynasty that men and boys were forced, under the threat of severe punishment, to wear their hair in queues: shaved scalps above the temples with long braided ponytails worn down their backs.

Many coolies worked on sugar plantations in Cuba or in guano pits in Peru. In these places, their story mimics those of many African slaves working plantations in the South before the Civil War—long days of hard labor, very little food and poor shelter, and physical consequences for the perception of any wrongdoing. Their journeys to their destinations, too, were similar to the wretched conditions aboard slave ships—coolies were packed in like animals with great numbers succumbing to death before the ships docked. Likewise, because of the difficult working conditions, many coolies died before reaching the end of their contracts and finding the freedom they sought.

Research suggests that Amos Peck had abolitionist (anti-slavery) leanings, which may explain why Amos brought the young Joseph home to his mother to be raised as a member of the family instead of treating him like a slave. Joseph grew up on a Connecticut farm and attended school with the Peck children: William, Matthew, and Alice. While onboard Amos's ship, the crew took to calling him "Joe." When he arrived in America in 1852, "Joe" adopted the surname of the president of the United States at the time, Franklin Pierce.

The Fourteenth Connecticut was engaged in all the battles featured in *Freedom for Me*. Although Joseph Pierce was not present for the action at Antietam and Fredericksburg, apparently due to illness, the accounts of the battles were true to the actions of the regiment. At Gettysburg, the Fourteenth Connecticut was heavily engaged as described. Its soldiers manned the skirmish line, and attacked and burned the Bliss Barn. The regiment was positioned near the famous "copse of trees" on Cemetery Ridge, repulsed Pickett's Charge, and captured many enemy battle flags.

There are two notable exceptions to the history of the Fourteenth Connecticut as told in this story. First, the regiment did not receive training on their weapons while at Camp Foote near Hartford. Instead, they were issued muskets as they began their march over the Long Bridge from Washington City, immediately after being reviewed by President Lincoln and his advisors. Second, the president's review was moved to later in the novel to a point in which the regiment had seen action in battle, and when the main character had deepened his understanding of the meaning of the war and his place in it, and had begun to develop friendlier relationships with his comrades.

After the war, Joseph Pierce settled in Meriden, Connecticut. Through a Peck family relative, he got an apprenticeship in the silver trade and spent the rest of his adult life working as a silver engraver with the Meriden Britannia Company and later the International Silver Company. He married Martha Morgan on November 12, 1876 when she was 18 and he was 34. The couple had four children: Sula Edna in 1879; Edna Bertha, who was stillborn in 1881; Franklin Norris in 1882; and Howard Benjamin in 1884. They were members of the Trinity Methodist Episcopal Church. By all accounts, Joseph was able to achieve the American Dream even as he persisted through difficulties on account of his race.

In 1882, after an 1870s economic downturn, Congress reacted to a public outcry against Chinese laborers working menial jobs in California, claiming that they were taking the jobs of whites. The result was the Chinese Exclusion Act, which prohibited Chinese migration to America and made it difficult for the

Chinese to become U.S. citizens.

In the 1880 census, Joseph listed his race as Chinese. Ten years later, however, when the Chinese Exclusion Act had been in force for several years and prejudice against the Chinese had worsened, he listed his race as Japanese, possibly to protect his family from persecution. Sadly, to maintain this ruse, Joseph was forced to cut his queue.

Joseph retired in 1914 after working for 46 years. On January 3, 1916, he died at his home at the age of 73. His obituary in the *Meriden Daily Journal* stated simply, "He had resided in this city for many years and was well known and liked." Martha Morgan Pierce died on March 10, 1926 at the age of 67. She is buried next to Joseph in Walnut Grove Cemetery in Meriden.

Ninety years after Joseph's death, members of Company F, 14th Regiment Connecticut Volunteer Infantry, conducted a ceremony to dedicate the installation of a Grand Army of the Republic marker at the gravesite of Corporal Joseph Pierce. This was an unusual undertaking, as described by Michael Kroll, superintendent of the cemetery. In a *Meriden Record-Journal* article published on July 30, 2006, he said, "He's a big part of the history of Meriden and should be recognized. There aren't many other dedications; Pierce is singled out for the uniqueness of his whole story."

The gravesite marker was commemorated by Irving David

Moy, a member of Company F, 14th Regiment, Connecticut Volunteer Infantry, Inc., a non-profit Civil War living history and preservation organization. A Chinese-American, Irving portrays Joseph in battle reenactments and tirelessly shares the story of Joseph Pierce with today's generation. Irving has played a key role in preserving Joseph's legacy and his part in America's storied history—even to Joseph's family. It is thanks, in part, to Irving that the Pierce "family secret" was illuminated and Joseph's descendants learned the details of their proud Chinese heritage.

The cover art *Freedom for Me: A Chinese Yankee* proudly features one of the surviving pictures of Joseph Pierce in his uniform. The photo is courtesy of Irving David Moy and its owner, Michael J. McAfee.

ACKNOWLEDGEMENTS

Thank you for reading *Freedom for Me: A Chinese Yankee*. Seeing this novel in print is the fulfillment of a lifelong dream. Ever since learning about Joseph Pierce, I have felt called to write this story. It is and always will remain close to my heart. I am eternally grateful to God, the Father, the Son, and the Holy Spirit, for his mighty love and support of my dream and my life.

I am also indebted to my husband, Michael. His belief in me has never wavered and that was never more true than when I was writing—and re-writing—this book. During the times when I doubted my ability to finish this novel or to find a publisher to bring it to the world, he would tell me in no uncertain terms to cut it out and get back to doing what I love. His tough love is of the most generous nature and I treasure it. Thank you for being my best friend. I love you.

To our children: Thomas, Ryan, and Michaela. I love you with all my heart. I am proud of each of you and the people you are growing up to be. I want to extend a special thanks to Tommy who was an early reader of this novel and whose support of me, the author, is unmatched. In a journey full of high points, I am most proud of being able to show my kids that dreams are attainable as long as you keep the faith, see setbacks as opportunities, and determine to move forward no matter what obstacles you encounter or how long it takes.

Thank you to my ever-encouraging parents, Gene and Diana, who raised me in faith and have always believed in me. There are shades of my parents' advice and love that show up in the characters of Joseph and Madeline Beck, especially the gift of freedom to be comfortable in the person God designed me to be. Their love sustained me when I struggled at times with being half-Chinese because I would never choose to be anyone else's daughter or change anything about that part of me.

To the rest of my family, including my grandmother, Alene, my wonderful in-laws, Tom and Terri, and my brothers, Scott and Rob, as well my brothers-and sisters-in-law, nieces and nephews, godchildren, and my wonderfully large family, I love you all. Your support of me and this novel has meant the world to me. Thank you for everything.

Thanks, too, to my aunt Michelle, who has always been more like a sister to me, and to my friends, especially Kim, Loricia, Jacki, and Jody for their friendship, love, and support through the years. I am also thankful for the faith-filled and loving community of Immaculate Heart of Mary Church.

To the wonderful team of authors, writers, editors, and proofreaders who helped me with their advice, skills, and constructive criticism along the way: Rick Robinson, Chuck Sambuchino, Cynthea Liu, Mark Davis, Michael McIrvin, Peggy Thomas, Michael McColley, and especially, Stephen Hall and Megan Cassidy Hall, the dynamic duo behind 5050 Press, who nurtured my dream and took a chance on my novel. I could not have found a better home or two better people to work with. Thank you.

A special thank you to Irving David Moy, my friend, and today's Joseph Pierce. He is a historian, Civil War reenactor, author, and a kind and gentle soul. He generously reviewed my book, helped me with historical facts and lent his expertise to help me create authentic descriptions of battle scenes and camp life. He has done everything he could to support this novel. Thank you, Irving.

I also want to thank the pioneers of Civil War Chinese research and those committed to sharing the soldiers' stories, especially Ruthanne Lum McCunn, Carol Shively, Alex Jay, Gordan Kwok and all who came before. For nurturing my love of the Civil War, my gratitude abounds for the late Bruce Catton, and for moving me with his narrative historical fiction, Jeff Shaara. To all the great teachers who nurtured my love of literature and American History, I sincerely appreciate it.

I wrote this book because I was moved by the story of Joseph Pierce. I hope that by fictionalizing his story for young readers, I am able to share an important part of the Civil War story so that young people today know and appreciate that there were Chinese Civil War soldiers and understand that the fight for freedom can take many forms.

Thank you for reading. If you liked this novel, I would greatly appreciate a review on Amazon or Goodreads. I would also love to hear from you. Please connect with me via my website, www.staciehaas.com, or via Twitter (@staciehaas) or Facebook (@authorstaciehaas). A curriculum guide is available for teachers and home-schooling parents on my website as well as 5050 Press. For school visits and author talks, please visit these sites as well.

Also Available From 50/50 Press:

Mary is a naïve twenty year old in 1945 when her high school sweetheart, Jack, returns to their small Indiana steel town wounded from World War II and makes her his bride. While Jack struggles to find his place in the world, Mary begins her own journey of self-discovery. Mary's Christmas letters track her children from toddling to adulthood, while also commenting on her marriage, her friendships, and the world around her-- advances in technology, the dawn of the nuclear age, the Cuban Missile Crisis, The Cold War, Vietnam, Woodstock, and more. Through disappointments, triumphs, dark moments of doubt and suspicion, loss of loved ones, and the lessons learned from hard experience, Mary's Christmas letters are a constant in an uncertain world. A part of the ritual of Christmas, these letters are a touchstone from which Mary takes strength and comfort.

Coming Spring 2018!

UNDERCOVER
CHEFS

TOP
SECRET

ERIN FRY

Three unlikely friends join forces to win a baking competition and save their school's culinary classroom. Isaac, a nationally-ranked runner; Jane, a shy artist; and J.C., a rebellious scooter rider—all have a secret passion for cooking. The promise of a cupcake contest lures them to an unusual classroom on the outskirts of campus. As they share friendship and a love for cooking, the pressures of the contest start to boil over—a recipe for disaster that could destroy their chances at winning! The heat is on, and Isaac, Jane and J.C. must figure out a way to salvage their cupcakes, save the culinary classroom from being demolished, and protect their secrets before the judges cast their final votes.

Made in the USA
Lexington, KY
13 November 2017